IRON MAN

HarperCollins®, ■®, and HarperEntertainment™ are trademarks of
HarperCollins Publishers.

Iron Man: Teen Novelization
Printed in the United States of America. No part of this book may be used
or reproduced in any manner whatsoever without written permission except
in the case of brief quotations embodied in critical articles and reviews.
For information address HarperCollins Children's Books, a division of
HarperCollins Publishers, 1350 Avenue of the Americas,
New York, NY 10019.
www.harpercollinschildrens.com

Library of Congress catalog card number: 2007938650
ISBN 978-0-06-082198-2

Typography by David Neuhaus

First Edition

IRON MAN

TEEN NOVELIZATION

By Dan Jolley

**Based on the screenplay by
Mark Fergus & Hawk Ostby
and
Art Marcum & Matt Holloway
Based on the Marvel comic**

▇ HarperEntertainment
An Imprint of HarperCollinsPublishers

Afghanistan. Today.

The U.S. military convoy crawled and scraped its way through some of the most forbidding terrain on Earth. The five Humvees were dwarfed by their surroundings. Jagged mountains as threatening as dagger blades loomed on the horizon. Some were miles away, across vast plains of blasted rock; others jutted from the ground only a few hundred yards from the dirt-and-gravel road.

The loud rock music blaring from the Humvee ahead of his did nothing to make Tony Stark feel any more at ease. He craned his neck to get a better look out the window, squinting as unforgiving sunlight flashed off the snow-capped peaks in the distance. The mountains seemed closer to the road the farther the convoy traveled, as if every vehicle in the line would eventually get wedged into a tiny canyon, or just run straight into a sheer rock wall.

Tony settled back into his seat. Everything about him announced his wealth. The cut of his thick, dark

5

hair and the meticulously groomed mustache and goatee added to the image, but it was Tony Stark's demeanor and piercing eyes that did the trick more than anything else.

"It's the way you look at people, Tony," an acquaintance had once said. "All you have to do is look at somebody, and they *know* you're smoother than they are, smarter than they are, you drive faster cars than they do and date better-looking women. And you don't have to say a word."

Tony glanced around at the three airmen in the Humvee with him. He could read the names on the uniforms for two of them: Ramirez and Pratt. The third sat at an angle to Tony with his name obscured, but Tony had heard someone call him "Jimmy."

Tony felt out of place, sitting there in his $10,000 Italian suit, but not unbearably so. He lifted the glass of champagne in his left hand and took a satisfying swallow.

The airmen simply sat there, the three of them with their weathered faces, as silent as statues.

The rock music from the other vehicle hit three heavy power chords and faded away, leaving only the rumble of the engines and the sound of the stones crunching beneath them.

Tony pointed at one of the airmen, his eyes mischievous. "I get it. You guys aren't allowed to talk. Is that it? Are you not allowed to talk?"

His tone was light, confident, shading into brash. A tiny smile that wasn't quite a smirk hovered on

6

Tony's lips as he took another drink from the crystal tumbler.

The airman called Jimmy grinned and fidgeted with an orange sports watch strapped around his left wrist. "No, we're allowed to talk."

Tony shifted in his seat, managing to look casual and suave at the same time. His tone stayed light when he said, "Oh. I see. So it's personal."

Jimmy's expression switched from nervous to embarrassed, and his gaze dropped to his feet.

Ramirez said, "I think they're intimidated," and the smooth contralto of her voice surprised Tony enough to make him check his grip on the glass.

"You're a woman!"

Ramirez's eyebrows lifted half an inch. None of the rest of her face changed as she regarded Tony with a stony, unamused gaze. Jimmy and Pratt both stifled laughter, Jimmy going so far as to cover his mouth with a fist and pretend to cough.

Amid the suppressed chuckles, Tony said, "I, hey, honestly, I couldn't have called that." He realized he was making the situation worse, but only shrugged, despite Ramirez's visibly mounting irritation. "I would apologize, but isn't that what we're going for here? I saw you as a soldier first."

Before Ramirez could respond, Jimmy jumped in. "I have a question, sir."

Tony made a languid gesture with one hand—the kind of gesture made by someone unconcerned by the little details of the world around him. "Please."

Jimmy's cheeks reddened as he asked, "Is it true you're twelve for twelve with last year's *Bolt* cover models?"

Tony ignored Ramirez's rolling eyes. "Excellent question. Yes and no. March and I had a schedule conflict but, thankfully, the Christmas cover was twins. Anyone else? You, with the hand up." He indicated Pratt.

Pratt said, "It's a little embarrassing."

With perfect composure, Tony responded, "Join the club."

Pratt cleared his throat. "Can I take a picture with you?"

Tony frowned. "Are you aware that Native Americans believe photographs steal a little piece of your soul?" Jimmy and Pratt both gave him blank looks. Tony let them hang for a second longer before he said, "Ah, not to worry, mine's long gone. Fire away."

Ramirez silently got out of the way as Pratt and Jimmy maneuvered around inside the Humvee. Jimmy held Pratt's camera—a green-and-white plastic disposable—as Pratt posed next to Tony, a ridiculous grin on the airman's face.

"Say cheese," Jimmy said, snapping the shutter.

"Do one more," Pratt urged, as Jimmy wound the film forward.

"Okay, okay. Ready? Three . . . two . . ."

Just as Jimmy began to say "one," the Humvee ahead of them erupted into a white-hot fireball.

The shock-wave knocked the nose of Tony's

Humvee into the air, cracked the windshield, and filled Tony's world with thunder and stabbing pain in his ears.

The Humvee dropped violently back to earth, shrapnel peppering it with thousands of tiny impacts. Tony's head cracked hard against the side window, his eyes only inches from the big sideview mirror, in which he saw the Humvee directly behind them explode in another sunlike ball of flame, the force of the detonation knocking it sideways, completely off the road.

Everything became shouts and screams and black, oily smoke and choking dust. Pratt gripped Tony's shoulder and suddenly transformed into a battle-hardened professional soldier. "Stay here!" he barked, and Tony could only nod as Pratt, Jimmy, and Ramirez scrambled out.

The Humvee's door slammed behind them, sealing Tony in. He moved over to the window, peering out, eyes wide as the airmen tried to move into a defensive formation . . . and then he saw Jimmy scream in shock, wide-eyed, as a dirt-crusted metal cylinder sprang up waist high from the ground in front of him.

Tony didn't have time to react, didn't have time to shout any kind of warning. He only had time to think the words *bouncing Betty* before the land mine went off, stitching Jimmy with shrapnel. Tony watched in horror as Jimmy's body slumped to the ground. Then he flinched back from the window as Lieutenant Colonel James Rhodes came running past, holding a .50 caliber

9

machine gun, his face streaked with dirt and sweat.

Several inches taller than Tony, his brown skin rippling with muscle, James Rhodes was Tony's closest friend, colleague, part-time handler, and full-time protector.

Tony screamed, *"Rhodey!"* just as Rhodes turned to look at him through the window.

"Get down, Tony," Rhodey bellowed. *"Get the—"* But an explosion cut him off, filling the air with even denser smoke and more billowing clouds of gritty dust.

Rhodey whirled and fired into the murk, then disappeared through the clouds as Tony watched, one hand pressed against the glass. Tony looked around, thinking quickly, trying to figure out the best course of action, when another Humvee exploded and the windows of Tony's vehicle gave way, showering him with fragments of safety glass. Tony shouted and lunged for the door . . . but conditions outside the vehicle were far worse than inside. Tony couldn't see more than three feet in any direction, and the world around him became one of machine-gun muzzle flashes, screams, and tracer bullets snapping past him like a swarm of alien insects.

Tony ducked down low and scampered away from the battered Humvee, past the wreckage of another. On the ground in front of him he spotted a discarded M-16 and grabbed it, but dropped it just as quickly. The weapon was burning hot, far too hot to touch, and Tony shook his hands, hoping they weren't blistered too badly.

10

He couldn't tell where anyone was, and when something bounced off the smoldering carcass of a Humvee nearby with a *pinging* sound, Tony jumped, badly startled. The object thudded in the dirt right behind him. He got closer, trying to get a good look at it . . . and when he did, the entirety of the universe seemed to narrow down to one diamond-hard point.

Tony was less than two feet away from a rocket-propelled grenade, the shining cylinder lying there in the Afghan sand, and on its side were the words USM 11676 – STARK MUNITIONS.

Tony not only identified the grenade immediately as one of his, but also recognized the batch; this one had come from the plant in Denver, Colorado. The information flashed through his mind at the same time that he was desperately trying to get his limbs to cooperate, trying to move, to get away, to at least throw himself to one side so as not to take the full brunt of the grenade when it went off . . . but he was too disoriented, too close to panic, and in exactly the wrong position to do any good.

The impact of the grenade's detonation blew Tony completely off his feet, shredding the Italian suit and revealing layers of Kevlar body armor underneath it.

Body armor that proved to be pitifully inadequate.

Memories mingled with reality as Tony Stark began the long, slow, painful climb out of unconsciousness and into the light. He knew this was no light of heaven or any other kind of afterlife. It was too bright. Even through his eyelids it hurt his eyes.

The ambush played and replayed in his head, and Tony spent awhile figuring out how much of what he was experiencing was real and how much was simply hallucinations. He saw the fireballs again, felt the heat . . . remembered the moment of impact as the grenade blew up in his face.

"Oh no, the shrapnel," he wanted to moan, or at least whisper to himself, but his vocal chords refused to work. Tony concentrated on separating fact from fiction, pushing the ambush away and focusing on what was around him right now.

His ears rang loudly. Did he hear voices? Wait, wait. One thing at a time.

Scents first—dirt, stagnant water. Stale sweat. . . . Machine oil?

Tony finally snapped awake as if resurfacing from a deep, dark pool, and with the consciousness came an awareness that something had gone terribly, horribly wrong with his body.

Tony gasped at the searing, ripping pain in his chest—*not the shrapnel, please, not the shrapnel*—and tried to touch the wound, but couldn't: His arms and legs were bound. Focusing his eyes took staggering effort, and he almost passed out again, but finally he managed to look down at himself.

Someone had tied him to a chair. He still had his pants on, but he'd been stripped from the waist up, and a bundle of blood-soaked bandages had been sloppily applied to his chest.

Tony knew what he was going to find underneath the bloody cloth. He could only approach the thought from a distance, at a sharp angle. If he considered it directly he knew he'd start screaming.

It finally registered that he was indeed hearing someone speak. Seconds later Tony identified the language: Dari, one of the tongues commonly spoken in Afghanistan. That's when the rest of his surroundings, and the awful reality of his situation, truly sank in.

Tony was sitting in a dank cave, staring at two Afghans, both of them flanking a digital video camera set up on a tripod. The lens stared at him like the unblinking eye of a Cyclops. Tony craned his neck around and felt his guts tighten with desperation.

A group of men stood behind him, all of them in hoods, all of them lined up before a huge banner displaying ten interlocking rings. Their leader stood poised at Tony's shoulder, a huge *Choori* knife in one hand, spouting rhetoric for the camera.

Tony had been taken prisoner.

And he was starring in his own ransom video.

Chapter One

Las Vegas. Two days ago.

Images danced across a huge screen, black-and-white and grainy: bombs falling from the sky, Japanese fighter planes diving and twisting, machine-gun bullets tracking across the hulls of burning, sinking battleships. The attack on Pearl Harbor unfolded as Franklin Delano Roosevelt made an impassioned speech in the background.

At a podium in front of the screen, Lieutenant Colonel James Rhodes spoke, his voice boosted by a microphone. "December 7, 1941: the day the world changed forever. President Roosevelt declares the United States will build fifty thousand planes to fight the armies of Hirohito and Hitler."

As Rhodey spoke, the images on the screen flowed into a montage. Goose-stepping Nazi SS officers. An American airplane hangar with a sign that read STARK INDUSTRIES. A slim young man shaking hands with FDR: Howard Stark. A sunset sky thick with long-range Stark bombers.

"Although no such capacity to build existed, Howard Stark, founder of the fledgling Stark Industries, answers his call to duty and builds not fifty, but a hundred thousand planes. Later, Stark's work on the Manhattan Project makes the end of the war possible. Stark Industries would go on to contribute to every major weapons system through the Cold War."

The screen shifted from images of intercontinental ballistic missiles and nuclear submarines to Howard Stark holding a tiny baby.

"But Howard Stark's greatest achievement would come in 1973. From early on, it was clear that young Tony Stark had a unique gift."

The screen flashed to Tony at age four, then at twelve, then in his late teens.

"At seventeen he graduated summa cum laude from MIT. Four years later, tragedy would pass the Stark mantle from father to son."

The image behind Rhodey cut to an elaborate funeral, with hundreds of mourners in attendance. Tony Stark stood near his father's coffin, gray-faced and hollow-eyed, flanked by George Bush Sr. and Bill Clinton.

"It was the loss of a titan. But Tony did not let personal grief distract him from his duty. At twenty-one, he became the youngest-ever CEO of a Fortune 500 company. And with it came a new mandate. Smarter weapons, fewer casualties. A dedication to preserving life."

The presentation ramped up toward its climax, as a

slickly produced display of American military might flashed across the screen: foot soldiers marching in formation, tanks crashing across a battlefield, planes launching into the sky.

"Today Tony Stark's ingenuity continues to protect freedom and American interests around the globe."

The screen image faded into an American flag waving dramatically in the wind, superimposed with a skillfully rendered photographic portrait of Tony Stark today: polished. Confident. Strikingly handsome and fiercely intelligent.

Thunderous applause swelled as that last image faded to black, and continued as a single spotlight sprang up and illuminated Rhodey standing at a podium, bold and dashing in a pin-striped suit.

"As Program Manager and Liaison to Stark Industries, I've had the honor of serving with a real patriot, a man whose life has been dedicated to protecting our troops on the front lines. He's a friend. And a great mentor. A man who has always been there for his friends and his country. Ladies and gentlemen, this year's Apogee Award winner—Mr. Tony Stark."

Deafening applause filled the room as, perfectly on cue, a second spotlight came on and shone down . . . on an empty chair.

The applause quickly petered out, and after a few seconds the house lights came on. Tony Stark's empty chair sat at the best table in the Grand Ballroom of the Las Vegas Caesar's Palace Hotel and Casino, surrounded by roughly a thousand people in black-tie, evening-gown chic.

It was an impressive crowd, if you knew who and what to look for. Military brass, politicians, lobby-ists—movers and shakers. Power brokers. All of them there to see one man.

Murmurs and whispers began to move across the floor, heads swiveling. *"Where's Tony?" "Was he delayed?" "He's not blowing this off, is he?"*

At a table adjacent to the one where Tony Stark was supposed to be sitting, Obadiah Stane quickly took the measure of the crowd and got to his feet.

Obadiah presented a striking figure, with his shaved-smooth scalp and silver goatee, but the way he moved and spoke gave off a very humble, earthy, *aw-shucks* kind of vibe. He was like everybody's favorite uncle—and that presence had served him well as Chief Financial Officer of Stark Industries over the years.

Obadiah nodded a little awkwardly to several members of the military as he made his way up to the podium. Rhodey gladly gave Obadiah space at the microphone, looking as if he had a few words he'd like to say himself. Obadiah shot Rhodey a sympathetic look before he addressed the gathered crowd.

"Thank you . . . I, uh, I'm not Tony Stark, but if I were, I'd tell you how honored I am and . . . what a joy it is to receive this award." Obadiah hesitated, trying not to freeze under all the impatient stares. "The best thing about Tony is also the worst thing: He's always working."

Chapter Two

At the precise moment when Obadiah Stane said, "He's always working," a pair of translucent red dice tumbled the length of a craps table and turned up seven.

The densely packed crowd around the table erupted with cheers and whoops. "Everybody wins!" the dealer announced, and both of the flawlessly beautiful women on either side of Tony Stark squealed and clapped. Tony grinned, smug, pleased with the roll but not surprised.

He'd been standing at the craps table for not quite half an hour, and this latest roll typified the luck he'd been having all night.

Tony leaned over to whisper in one woman's ear. She saw him moving closer, gave him a perfect, wet-lipped smile, and brushed her hair back over one ear to be sure she heard him clearly.

"You think we're having a 'moment,' here," Tony

said, "but this is actually the logical conclusion of several mathematical truisms."

She batted her lashes at him. "Oh?"

He continued, his tone casual but with unshakable confidence. "Your hypothalamus is flooding your system with a chain of proteins called peptides, so that every cell in your body is opening itself up to the happy chemical: oxytocin."

It took a rare breed to pull off the kind of patter Tony was speaking, a rare breed possessed of equal combinations of intellect, education, and guts. Tony had all three in abundance.

The woman seemed to like the idea of getting closer to Tony Stark. Practically purring, she said breathily, "That's . . . wow . . ."

The dice in his hand again, Tony said, "Hold on a second." He shook them, rolled—and the crowd cheered again, deafeningly this time.

Tony slid his arm around the woman's slim waist, his eyes flashing. "So now your limbic system is positively . . . throbbing. A Kirlian photograph of us right now, occupying this space, would show serious subatomic particles being exchanged between us, with a rapidity that transcends—"

He paused. The woman had pressed herself against him, her eyelids lowered, biting her bottom lip seductively. Tony's arm didn't move from around her waist, but he took on a playful tone when he said, "Are you getting this? You *will* be quizzed."

Then something caught Tony's eye over the

woman's head, and the playfulness faded rapidly. Rhodey made his way through the crowd, glowering, on a collision course for Tony. People took one look at Rhodey's expression and moved out of his way.

Tony released the woman as Rhodey stopped in front of him. "They roped you into this thing, too?"

Rhodey narrowed his eyes a fraction of an inch. In a voice as dry as dust, he said, "Yeah. They said you'd be deeply honored if I presented."

Tony shrugged, resigned. "Okay. Let's do it."

His hand not quite trembling with anger, Rhodey thumped the Apogee Award statue down on the felt of the craps table.

Tony barely reacted. As he spoke, he turned back to the table, scanning the bets. "That was quick. Thought there'd be more of, you know, a ceremony. Maybe a highlight reel . . ."

He shook the dice. All eyes on him. He rolled . . . and crapped out.

The crowd groaned, most of them eyeing Rhodey with mixtures of anger and resentment. Still unfazed, Tony spoke to the boxman. "Color me up." Then, to the crowd, he said, "My chaperone has just arrived with my"—he hefted the trophy carelessly—"Degenerate of the Year award. Judging from his look, I may have just peed in the kiddie pool."

The boxman racked up Tony's chips. Despite the loss, his winnings were considerable. Tony continued, "I must now take my leave, along with the House's funds."

He took the heavy rack of chips, tipped the table operators with ridiculous generosity, blew a cavalier kiss to the beautiful, nameless woman, and headed away from the table with Rhodey. The woman watched him go wistfully, but didn't try to follow.

As they moved through the casino, the degree of Tony's celebrity made itself felt. Security guards fell in behind them without being instructed to. Casino patrons did double-takes, tugged on companions' elbows and pointed, and snapped pictures of him with their camera phones.

Tony either didn't notice or pretended not to.

Not looking at Tony, Rhodey said, "A lot of people would kill to have their name on that award."

"It belongs to my old man," Tony replied dismissively. "They should have given it to him."

Rhodey frowned. "What's wrong with you? A thousand people came here tonight to honor you, and you leave them with egg on their faces. This award means something, Tony, it's bigger than you—"

Tony cut him off. "Hold that thought a sec." They were coming up on a roulette table; Tony stopped and set his rack of chips down. "Put it all on black," he told the operator. "Don't worry—it's approved."

Instantly a crowd gathered, drawn to the unthinkably extravagant bet like sharks to a wounded seal. Rhodey glanced around at them uncomfortably, but none of them paid him any mind. Every ounce of their attention was focused solely on the heavy rack of chips and the wheel just beyond it.

The operator spun the wheel without question. The ball whirred around the rim, dropped in, bounced . . . and settled on red.

The operator scooped away the heavy rack as Tony watched bemusedly.

The crowd didn't breathe for several seconds. Then they let out a collective sigh—the kind of sigh that carries hopes and dreams with it—and drifted away from the table.

His voice brittle, Rhodey said, "You just blew three million dollars."

Tony shoved his hands in his pockets. "Yeah. Don't know what was more exciting, winning it or the fact that I don't care I just lost it."

"Everything's funny to you."

"No. *You're* not funny."

Rhodey rolled his eyes. "We've got quite a day tomorrow. Can we get out of here now?"

"One more stop."

Minutes later, Rhodey stood at one of the sinks in a huge, ornate bathroom. He could barely hear the sounds of the casino floor outside. Aside from Tony and himself, the bathroom was empty.

Tony's voice echoed out of one of the stalls as Rhodey splashed his face with water. "Of course I respect your opinion."

Rhodey dried off with a plush towel, his expression dour. "This is no joke. You're going into a hot zone. We should be doing this test here in Nevada."

Tony's expertly shined shoes were the only part of him visible below the stall door. Rhodey heard the sound of toilet paper unrolling. "This system has to be demonstrated in true field conditions," Tony said.

Rhodey turned and leaned against the sink, his arms folded across his chest, and was about to respond when the bathroom door swung open and a stunning woman walked in.

Take 30 percent schoolmarm, 30 percent drop-dead gorgeous blue-eyed blond bombshell, and 40 percent Harvard MBA valedictorian, mix them together, and the result was Tony Stark's personal assistant.

Virginia "Pepper" Potts had worked for Tony for the last seven years, during which time she had developed a number of signature traits.

First, her hair was always perfectly arranged in a slick, conservative, all-business style. Second, her cell phone never left her and was usually accessorized with a tiny earpiece. Third, Pepper kept Tony's entire life on a tablet computer that rarely strayed from her hands.

Her clothes never had any wrinkles, always displayed the utmost in both fashion and taste, and almost—but not quite—hid the lithe, lean body underneath them.

Rhodey showed no sign of surprise that Pepper was in the men's room. They nodded to each other, business as usual. Pepper had her cell phone in her hand, open and in use, her tablet PC tucked under one arm.

"Tony, it's the president. Wants to congratulate

you personally. Heads up." She tossed the phone over the top of the stall.

Tony's voice switched to professional mode—or at least, as professional as Tony Stark got. "Jim, how're the trout running?" Rhodey shook his head as Tony continued. One of the spotless black shoes visible under the stall door tapped merrily to an unheard rhythm "Yeah, sitting on top of the world here. Working on my masterpiece . . ."

Minutes later, after Tony had finished with all of his business—personal and otherwise—and Pepper had the cell phone back, Tony washed his hands and started to follow Rhodey out of the bathroom. Rhodey dropped a few bills into the absent attendant's tip basket.

Tony motioned to his two companions and said, "After you." Then, with Rhodey's and Pepper's backs turned, Tony added the Apogee Award to the basket.

He emerged onto the casino floor—completely ignoring the long line of patrons waiting to get into the bathroom, all of them cordoned off by security until Tony had finished—and caught up with Rhodey and Pepper.

"You're leaving the country for a week," Pepper said to him, still all business. "I need five minutes."

"Okay. Shoot."

The three of them exited the casino. Tony headed straight for his waiting limo, with Rhodey and Pepper doggedly following him. The limo had attracted a crowd, which security held at bay. Tony ignored them with practiced ease.

Pepper checked her tablet PC and said, "The board meeting is on the eleventh. Should I tell them to expect an appearance?"

Tony paused, about to answer, then allowed himself to be distracted by a feminine voice.

"Mr. Stark!"

He scanned the crowd and quickly pinpointed the voice's owner: a shapely brunette holding a voice recorder. She struggled to get closer to him while security held her back. "Mr. Stark!" she called again. "Christine Everhart, journalist. Can I ask you a few questions?"

Tony let one corner of his mouth twitch upward. "Can I ask a few back?"

Everhart gave him the kind of smile that would make most men weak at the knees. Tony signaled to security; once free of their grip, she gave her clothes a quick, smoothing pass and walked over to him.

Pepper shook her head in an unknowing parody of the gesture Rhodey had made in the casino bathroom, and might have said something if her cell phone hadn't rung. She took the call as Christine Everhart spoke to Tony, holding up the recorder.

"You've been described as a da Vinci for our times. What do you say to that?"

Without batting an eye, Tony replied, "Ridiculous. I don't paint."

Everhart's sparkling eyes took on a tiny malicious glint. "And what do you say to your other nickname: 'The Merchant of Death'?"

He thought about it for half a second. "That's actually not bad . . ."

It became clear in an instant that approaching this topic with humor was *not* going to win any points with the reporter, as her eyes went from fiery to ice-cold. Tony's eyebrows raised a little. "Let me guess. Berkeley?"

She replied flatly: "Brown."

He shoved his hands in his pockets, unperturbed. "Well, Miss Brown, it's an imperfect world, and I assure you that the day weapons are no longer needed to keep the peace, I'll start manufacturing bricks and beams to make baby hospitals."

Now the ice moved into her voice. "Rehearse that much, Mr. Stark?"

"Every night in front of the mirror. Call me Tony."

Everhart held the recorder in front of her like a weapon. "I'm sorry, *Tony,* I was hoping for a serious answer."

"Here's serious. My old man had a philosophy: Peace means having a bigger stick than the other guy."

She almost scoffed. "Good line, coming from the guy selling the sticks."

Despite himself, Tony started getting serious. "My father helped defeat Hitler. He was on the Manhattan Project. A lot of people—including your professors at Brown—might call that being a hero."

Her expression didn't change. "Others might call it war-profiteering."

Tony stared at her for a heartbeat, responses running

through his head one after another . . . and then he grinned. He couldn't help it in the face of her single-minded onslaught. "Tell me: do you plan to report on the millions we've saved by advancing medical technology? Or kept from starving with our intelli-crops? All were breakthroughs spawned from, that's right, military funding."

"Wow. You ever lose an hour of sleep your whole life?"

They stood staring at each other, Tony wasn't sure for how long, while Rhodey and Pepper stood waiting in the wings. Christine Everhart clearly wasn't about to back down. Not that he wanted her to.

Chapter Three

The bedside clock shifted from 5:59 to 6:00, but it wasn't anything as simple as an alarm going off that awakened Christine in Tony's bed. She opened her eyes, blinking sleep away, and frowned as the floor-to-ceiling windows that made up the entire west wall began to shift from dark . . . to translucent . . . to clear.

Christine sat up, eyes wide, and dragged the sheet with her as she walked to the window. The TV flickering to life off to her right startled her, but didn't distract her from taking in the scenery.

Tony Stark's estate, a mammoth, sprawling monument to cutting-edge architecture and mind-boggling wealth, would have been impressive enough on its own. Indeed, Christine *had* been impressed, the night before, when she arrived here with Tony in the limo that had picked them up from the airport. But to add this to the mix . . . she had no words for it.

Tony's home perched impossibly high atop a set of cliffs overlooking the Pacific Ocean. It was this vista that greeted Christine as she stared far down and far-ther out, to the ends of the earth.

A seagull flew past the window. Christine giggled, delighted.

Finally she turned away from the window and padded over to the closet, intent on greeting Tony in one of his own shirts. But the door wouldn't open, even when she rattled the knob and pulled hard. She whispered, "Who locks their closet?"

Then she almost jumped out of her skin as the television spoke to her. "I'm sorry, Miss Everhart, you are not authorized to access that area."

Freaked out, Christine scrambled for cover, coming up with the shirt Tony had worn the previous night on the plane. She barely got the garment over her head, when the door opened and Pepper walked in, already dressed in perfect business attire and holding dry-cleaned clothes wrapped in plastic.

Pepper indicated the TV with a small gesture. "Don't worry, that's Jarvis—he runs the house. Jarvis: deactivate security." She cast an eye carefully devoid of expression at Tony's shirt, comically oversized on Christine's body. "Here, Miss Everhart—your clothes, cleaned and pressed. Anything else I can get you?"

Christine hesitated, a bit rattled by the creepy TV-voice and Pepper's unexpected arrival. She stood up straight and tried to rally, addressing Pepper as if she were domestic help. "Look, Tony wanted me to stay for breakfast, but I've got to get a jump on the day. Call me a cab, would you?"

Pepper didn't quite smile. "Cab's waiting outside."

That round went to Pepper, but Christine wasn't done playing. "And a coffee, hon. Black. One Splenda."

Pepper gave her a sweet smile. "Should I tell Mr. Stark you were satisfied with the interview?"

Wordlessly, Christine picked up her clothes and stalked off into the bathroom.

As Christine Everhart climbed into the waiting taxi, Tony Stark sighed and stretched and looked around at a space the size of a small aviation hangar built beneath his mansion.

It was Tony's private, in-home workshop: part little-boy fantasy, part auto garage, part mad scientist's lair.

Tony loved this place.

Constructed beneath the foyer and living room of the main house, the primary work floor was both enormous and insanely crowded. Gone was the precision with which the teenage Tony had laid out the parts of the turbine engine; this scene, if it mirrored any state of mind, was one of confusion and chaos.

In one corner sat a tangle of ultramodern unmanned flight drones in various stages of disassembly, surrounded by parts from six different types of missiles. The jumble spilled out across the floor, mingling at the far end with sports cars both modern and vintage, as well as a chaotic profusion of long-abandoned prototypes. These puzzling machines ranged from weapon-deployment racks to something that looked like a cross between an X-wing fighter and a soda machine.

Soft music drifted through the workshop, originating from an old Wurlitzer jukebox in the far corner, but piped through a top-of-the-line speaker array built discreetly into all four walls.

Above the main workbench, framed photos (kept spotlessly clean) showed a young Tony and his father, Howard, the two of them working on a 1932 Ford. An array of computer monitors near the photos ran AutoCAD images of a flathead engine.

And right in the middle of the workshop was Tony Stark, wearing a white undershirt and suit slacks, working on the same '32 Ford from the photograph. Smears of grease and oil dotted his clothing and his skin. A glimmer of the same happiness Tony had felt as a teenager came through on his face . . . but just a glimmer.

Pepper walked into the workshop, busy on her tablet PC. She spared Tony a glance. "You still owe me five minutes."

He didn't stop working. "Five? I'll need a bit longer than that—"

"Focus," Pepper said, cutting him off. "I need to leave on time today."

"You're rushing me. What, you have plans tonight?"

She made a tiny, frustrated sound. "The MIT commencement. Yes or no?"

"Maybe. Tell me your plans."

"I'll tell them 'yes.' You want to buy the Jackson Pollock? There is another buyer in the wings."

Tony reached for a socket wrench. "What's it look like?"

"It's a minor work in his later spring period, it's ludicrously overpriced—"

"Buy it."

Pepper's cell phone rang. She tapped her earpiece and took the call, listened, and then said, "He left an hour ago. Okay." She ended the call and said, "It's Rhodey again."

Tony finally stopped working on the Ford and eyed Pepper speculatively. "You *do* have plans, don't you?"

"I'm allowed to have plans on my birthday."

"It's your birthday again?"

Her tone neutral, Pepper said, "Yep. Funny, same day as last year."

"Huh." Tony picked up the socket wrench again. "Well, get yourself something from me. Something nice."

"Already did."

He raised his eyebrows. "And?"

"It was very tasteful, very elegant. Thank you, Mr. Stark."

"You're welcome, Miss Potts."

Tony went back to work on the Ford as Pepper left the workshop.

An hour and forty-five minutes later, Lieutenant Colonel James Rhodes paced back and forth in front of a Stark Industries business jet in the Stark Aviation hangar at the Santa Monica Airport. He wore his dress uniform and spoke sharply into a cell phone, impatience coming through loud and clear in his body language.

Rhodey was just about to raise his voice when a distant rumble made him pause. He squinted into the distance, down the length of the road leading to the hangar, and hit the phone's "END" button, his face creased with annoyance and frustration.

The rumble grew louder and louder, until an Audi R8 rocketed into the hangar. The car screeched to a stop in front of him and revved its engine.

Rhodey dropped his phone into a pocket and folded his arms, his expression frosty.

The Audi stayed there, doors shut tight, engine revving.

Seconds later, while the Audi's engine continued showing off, a limousine followed the smaller car's path into the hangar and pulled to a stop beside it. The limo's trunk popped open, and Hogan, Tony's usual driver, got out and retrieved a single overnight suitcase from it.

Having obviously waited for this so that he could scoot right onto the plane—thereby skirting the tongue-lashing he knew Rhodey had prepared for him—Tony opened the Audi's door and jumped out. He headed straight for the plane, breezing past the lieutenant colonel.

"Sorry, pal," Tony said nonchalantly. "Car trouble."

Rhodey followed Tony onto the plane without a word.

In the main cabin, Rhodey settled into one of the plush leather seats, staring the proverbial daggers at Tony. "I was standing out there three hours!"

Tony sat down across from him. He didn't look Rhodey in the eyes. "Like I said. I had car trouble."

Rhodey took a breath to say something else, but at that moment a leggy, smiling flight attendant appeared at their side, holding out hot towels on silver-plated tongs.

Tony gave her a grin just a hair shy of lazy. "Thanks, maybe later."

Rhodey grabbed one of the towels and pressed it against his face. The plane vibrated slightly as the engines started up, their whine steadily building.

Neither man said another word until the plane was in the air. The silence continued until they had climbed to cruising altitude, and even then it took the flight attendant's return to spark anything like conversation.

"Would you like a drink, Mr. Stark?" she asked silkily, leaning forward just enough to flash a generous amount of cleavage.

"Two fingers of whiskey." Tony dragged his eyes away from the attendant and, not quite grudgingly, asked Rhodey, "You want one?"

Rhodey didn't stop to think about it. "We're working."

Tony shrugged. "You should have a drink. We've

got a twelve-hour flight ahead of us."

An unsubtle note of impatience in his voice, Rhodey said, "It's two in the afternoon."

"It's two in the *morning* where we're going. C'mon, ten hours 'bottle to throttle'—"

Rhodey grumbled, "Don't start with me," but the impatience had run its course, and Tony's charm began to work its magic again. They'd been friends too long, Rhodey supposed, for him to stay mad. Despite himself, Rhodey was starting to see Tony Stark, his good friend, rather than Tony Stark, the jerk who'd kept him waiting for no good reason.

Still, he saw no reason to start drinking in the middle of the day.

Tony persisted. "Jeez, we're not getting hammered. Just a nightcap. We'll sleep better, arrive fresh. It's the responsible thing to do. I don't know about you, but I want to sell some weapons."

Rhodey shook his head, his resolve firm.

At least I made it till the sun went down, Rhodey thought to himself, taking another sip of the rum and Coke in his left hand. He had sunk down into the leather chair, loosened his tie, and, as the saying went, was feeling no pain.

Rhodey shook his head, trying to get his thoughts back in order. "You don't get it. I don't work for the military because they paid for my education, or my father's education. Don't cheapen it like that."

Tony ran a finger casually around the rim of his

glass. "All I said was, with your smarts and your engineering background, you could write your own ticket in the private sector. On top of which, you wouldn't have to wear that straitjacket."

"*Straitjacket?* This uniform means something. A chance to make a difference. You don't respect that, because you don't understand."

Rhodey truly believed this; it wasn't just talk. He considered Tony his closest, best friend, ever since the two of them met while attending MIT. But the fact remained that Tony couldn't wrap his head around the concepts Rhodey held so dear.

Tony gestured with his chin toward one of the attractive flight attendants. "See that one? *Her* I understand."

Rhodey scowled and stared at his drink. "You're not listening to a word I'm saying."

"I *am* listening. And I'm changing the subject. It's the same litany every time you've had a thimble of alcohol. Drink One: reflections on the New American Century and related topics—"

The charm had abruptly worn off for Rhodey, but he tried not to be too severe, even through his rum-flavored haze. "Something's . . . seriously wrong with you, man."

Either oblivious or unconcerned, Tony continued. "Drink Two: a history of World War Two and the Tuskegee Flyers. Drink Three—"

Rhodey set his drink in a cup holder and unbuckled his seat belt. "I'm not talking to you anymore." He stood up and pushed past both Tony and the flight attendants, looking for somewhere else to sit.

Tony kept his eyes on the women as he called after Rhodey. "Go hang with the pilot. You'll get along, he's got a personality just like yours."

Halfway to the cockpit, Rhodey defiantly said, "Oh, yeah? I *will*." He moved quickly to the cockpit door, pulled it open—and found himself looking at two empty pilot chairs. The lights of a fully automated pilot system glimmered across the cockpit's instrumentation.

Tony glanced up as Rhodey returned to his seat and dropped into it. His tone as dry as dust, Rhodey said, "That's funny."

Equally deadpan, Tony asked, "You could tell?"

Chapter Four

The Stark Industries jet came in for a smooth landing at Bagram Air Force Base in northeastern Afghanistan. Watching the terrain out the window, Tony was struck by how *beige* everything looked. Beige earth. Beige buildings, beige tents. Beige planes and Jeeps. He decided it was a little like looking at an old sepia-toned photograph, except bleaker and more intimidating.

Tony looked fresh and well rested, despite the fact that he hadn't slept very well. Not a hair was out of place. Not one wrinkle marred his expensive suit.

When the door opened and the stairway descended, Tony bounded off the plane, down the stairs, and greeted the waiting line of military brass, both American and Afghan. With his most professional smile in place and his handshake at its firmest, Tony was "on." Ready to go.

Ready to sell.

Rhodey couldn't say the same, unfortunately. He

appeared in the doorway of the plane, his dress uniform replaced by the head-to-toe camouflage, weary and squinting even behind dark sunglasses. He peered over the shades, his blinking eyes filled with sleep, and took in the most noticeable features of the scene before him.

In the distance, a gigantic military jet sat on the airstrip, its cargo ramp open at the rear. Between the jet and the dour-faced officers Tony was talking to, a flatbed transport carried three Jericho missiles, clearly off-loaded from the military plane.

Without joy, Rhodey muttered, "Showtime."

The heavy, bone-shaking chatter of an NRF 425 machine gun filled the desert air as the man-shaped target dummy flew into pieces.

Tony, Rhodey, and the assembled military officers they had come to meet all stood or perched in and around a test site two miles from Bagram. The generals sat on folding chairs behind a safe-zone of sandbags and massive HESCO barricades, while a mix of Air Force security men and Afghan soldiers patrolled the perimeter.

Among the Air Force soldiers were three named Pratt, Ramirez, and a fresh-faced young man who insisted everyone call him Jimmy.

A jagged ridge of mountains to the northwest cast long, knifelike shadows across the rocky ground.

A safe distance away, but easily visible from where the officers sat, one of the Jericho missiles had been loaded into a mobile launcher. It rested there ominously, a motionless promise of destruction.

Tony eyed the obliterated target dummy, satisfied with his marksmanship, and set the machine gun down on a table next to a neatly arranged row of assault rifles and automatic shotguns. Then he turned to the American and Afghan leadership and launched into his sales pitch, strutting like a carnival barker.

Standing behind the generals, Rhodey rolled his eyes. There was no stopping Tony once he put on his pitchman persona.

"The age-old question," Tony began. "Is it better to be feared or respected? I say, is it too much to ask for both?"

Making sure he had the attention of every one of the military men in front of him, Tony gestured toward the nearby missile. "With that in mind, I humbly present the crown jewel of Stark Industries' Freedom Line. It's the first missile system to incorporate my proprietary Repulsor Technology. They say the best weapon is one you never have to fire. I prefer the one you only have to fire once."

Tony picked up a small triggering device and thumbed a button. The Jericho roared to life and shot into the sky. "That's how Dad did it, it's how America does it, and so far it has worked out pretty well. Find an excuse to fire off one of these, and I personally guarantee the enemy is not gonna want to leave their caves."

The missile was still visible, though only barely, a

tiny speck high in the western sky. Just as Tony finished speaking, the warhead burst apart into dozens of tiny, brilliantly glowing mini-missiles. The smaller projectiles appeared to be targeting the crest of the nearby mountain range and Tony positioned himself in exactly the right spot, at exactly the right angle. As he raised his arms, the assembled brass saw the missiles and the mountain range directly behind Tony, as if they had been framed by a gifted cinematographer.

"For your consideration," Tony called out, his voice ringing, and spread his hands dramatically. "The Jericho!"

Precisely on cue, the mini-missiles struck the ridge's crest, and the entire mountain range seemed to explode, the force of the blast was so powerful. A roiling, blinding wave of dust, propelled by the missiles' shock wave, washed down and across Tony, obscuring him and blinding the officers.

Speaking from somewhere inside the dust cloud, Tony said, "Now there's one last creation I haven't shown anyone yet." The dust thinned and finally settled enough for Tony to be visible again. A large silver case had appeared on the table next to the assault rifles. Tony opened it, releasing wisps of dry-ice vapor.

The officers leaned forward, eyes on the case, intent on the secret it held. Tony reached inside and pulled out a bottle, followed by champagne flutes. He began pouring drinks for the military officials.

Several of them exchanged puzzled glances, unsure of what to make of this display. Tony's enthusiasm was undimmed, though, and he raised his glass triumphantly. "To peace, gentlemen. And with every five hundred million, I'll throw in a free one of these."

Once the presentation had wrapped up, all the armaments packed away, Tony and Rhodey watched the generals as the military men climbed into their Humvees and departed to the east. The two of them walked over to their own convoy of waiting Humvees, ready to head out toward the west.

As they walked, Tony pulled a video phone out of his pocket and hit a number on speed dial. After a few rings, the screen lit up with Obadiah Stane's face. Obadiah's beard looked rumpled.

"Hey," Tony said. "What are you doing up?"

"Sleeping. How did it go?"

"I think we have an early Christmas coming."

"Sounds good." Obadiah's alertness seemed to be fading.

"Hey, why aren't you wearing the pj's I got you?"

His eyelids drooping, Obadiah mumbled, "I don't do monograms. I'm hanging up now, bye-bye."

The phone's screen went dark. Tony hit "END" and dropped it back in his pocket. "All right, who wants to ride with me? How about you three? Jimmy? It's Jimmy, right?"

Excited, but trying not to show it, Jimmy said, "Me?" Tony nodded and waved toward the truck, and Jimmy and the two other soldiers piled into Tony's Humvee.

Rhodey saw what was happening and shot Tony a bemused glance.

"Sorry, Rhodey," Tony called out to him, "no room for my conscience in here. Or that hangdog look." He raised his glass of champagne. "See you back at base."

Rhodey shook his head silently and headed for another Humvee. As he passed one that was already full, someone inside cranked up a boom box, blasting loud rock music out into the desert air.

Chapter Five

Tony Stark awoke in hell.

Nightmare monsters and fever-dream lights loomed and danced, speaking in demonic words and phrases that Tony couldn't understand. They were tearing him apart, slowly, one shred of muscle and skin at a time, and interwoven between his body and his mind was *pain*. Ripping, burning, soul-destroying pain, as the demons slowly, deliberately pulled his heart from his chest.

Tony tried to speak, but could only manage a pitiful little groan. He wanted to make his arms and legs move, push himself up off this altar of agony, get the hell out of here, but something held him in place. Restraints? What was going on? Where *was* he? Tony panted and forced his eyes open.

Harsh light stabbed at him and made him blink, and at first he could only see bits and pieces at a time: a red scalpel. Blood-spattered hands.

Some kind of metal plate.

Black, glaring eyes.

Tony cranked his head, forced his chin down, and looked at his chest, which had been shredded, gouged, all but destroyed.

Tony looked around, wild, desperate, and finally made out the face of the man standing over him.

Performing surgery on him.

Thin. Dark complexion, receding hair. In his sixties. Tony tried to force his throat to work, tried to form words as he stared up at the man, but the surgeon barked out something in Arabic. Immediately rough hands grabbed Tony's head, yanked it back down against the table, and shoved a chloroform-soaked rag over his nose and mouth.

Everything went away, borne on sweet, thick, cloying clouds.

Tony flickered awake.

The harsh lights were gone. He lay on a cot on the floor of the cave, an IV plugged into his arm and a plastic tube protruding from his nose. Thick bandages covered his chest. He looked around, trying to get his bearings.

The first thing he saw was the surgeon, close by, not even ten feet away. The man stared into a broken mirror propped on a rock, humming a tune as he shaved with an old safety razor. Tony's attention drifted past the older man, though, and settled on a sight more precious than gold or diamonds right now: a jug of water resting on the "operating table."

Almost within reach.

Tony tried again to speak and couldn't. His eyes narrowed in frustration as he reached up, grabbed the nasal tube, pulled—and his gagging got worse as a good two feet of the tube slithered out of his nose.

Tony collapsed back onto the cot, already exhausted. Weakly, he croaked out, "Water . . . water . . ."

If the surgeon heard him, he gave no outward indication. He just kept humming the tune and slowly shaving.

Tony took hold of the IV and yanked it out of his arm. Then he rolled halfway onto his side and reached for the jug—but as he stretched, something attached to his chest snapped taut and stopped him. Tony looked down, trying to figure out what it could be. *Maybe it's another IV*, he thought.

But instead of an IV tube he saw a *wire* coming out from underneath his chest bandages. He followed it with his eyes, growing more horrified by the millisecond.

The wire anchored to his chest was hooked up to a car battery resting on the ground a couple of feet to his left.

Tony started clawing at the chest bandages, peeling and tearing, frantic to get them off, to know, to *see*.

The bandages came away, revealing the metal plate he'd spotted earlier, when he was half-delirious. The metal plate was now surgically attached to his chest, its edges sunken into his skin, tiny drops of blood oozing up from around it.

The sight proved too much. Tony passed out, sinking deep down into the darkness.

More vague, shadowy impressions. Fire dancing on metal; grunts and swears as men muscled huge, heavy objects across the cave floor; familiar smells. Grease. Machine oil.

Tony opened his eyes. His cot had been moved farther into the cave. Someone had built a sturdy-looking metal wall across the cave's exit tunnel, sealing them inside; a door with a sliding observation slat was set into the center of the wall and looked just as solid as its surroundings.

From where he lay, Tony could see a large furnace with flames flickering inside it. He also got the vague impression of large, crude metalworking implements nearby, but he wasn't paying attention to them yet.

The surgeon stood next to the furnace, stirring a battered metal pot set on top of it, inside which something bubbled and steamed. The older man glanced at Tony.

Tony raised himself to his elbows and dropped his gaze to his chest—and to the bulky metal plate that protruded now from fresh bandages.

"What have you done to me?"

Tony meant the question to come out with a lot more power.

The surgeon turned to face him. "What did I do? I removed what I could, but there's a lot left, headed for your atrial septum. Do you want a souvenir?" He picked up a glass jar from a nearby shelf and tossed it to Tony, who managed to catch it awkwardly.

The jar rattled and pinged as it landed. Tony took a good look at the scores of tiny, bloody barbs inside it, each one shaped like a lethal, razor-edged Christmas tree.

The surgeon said, "I've seen many wounds like this in my village. 'The walking dead,' we called them, because it took a week for the barbs to reach vital organs. I anchored a magnetic suspension system to the plate. It's holding the shrapnel in place . . . at least for now."

The color drained from Tony's face as the gravity of his situation sank in.

The surgeon continued matter-of-factly. "The barbs are lodged around your heart, Mr. Stark. If the magnetic plate loses power, they will begin to move. How long will it take for them to pierce the cardiac muscle and cause you to die of massive internal hemorrhaging? I can't say."

He lifted the spoon from the pot, blew on it, and took an experimental taste. "I am not without sympathy for your situation. I simply cannot help but appreciate the symmetry—the weapon designer cut down by his own creation. That grenade, those barbs, they *are* a Stark design, yes?"

Tony didn't answer. He set the jar aside, struggled to sit up, and did a double-take when he noticed the surveillance camera mounted on the cave wall.

The surgeon said, "That's right, smile."

Tony scowled.

The older man continued. "We met once, you and I. At a technical conference in Bern. My name is Yinsen."

Tony carefully observed the wire sprouting from his chest plate, gauging the length of it. "I don't remember."

"You wouldn't. If I'd been that drunk, I wouldn't have been able to stand, much less give a talk on integrated circuits."

Tony looked Yinsen in the eye. "Where are we?"

At that moment, the door flew open and a pair of dark, hostile eyes stared in at them. Yinsen dropped his spoon into the pot and put his hands on his head.

"Stand up!" he hissed. "Do as I do. Now!"

Tony understood the urgency of the situation and did the best he could to comply, but while he did manage to get to his feet—barely—he didn't have the strength to lift his arms above his head. Yinsen stepped over and helped him.

"Listen to me," the older man said, still in a harsh whisper. "Whatever they ask you, refuse. You understand? You must refuse."

The door opened, and three Arab men stepped into the cave, all of them in faded, worn military uniforms. Two held guns. The third Tony recognized from his body language: this was the leader, the man with the big knife who had stood next to Tony's chair during the recording of the ransom video. He wasn't a huge man, this leader, but Tony recognized the viciousness in his eyes.

Then he spotted Jimmy's orange watch on the wrist of one of the henchmen. Tony's jaw muscles clenched and rippled.

The leader began speaking in Dari. Yinsen translated: "He says, welcome, Tony Stark, the greatest mass murderer in the history of America. He is very honored."

The leader looked Tony up and down appraisingly, as if eyeing a prize horse, and spoke again. As he talked, he held out a photograph: a surveillance image of the Jericho missile launch.

Translating again, Yinsen said, "You will build for him the Jericho missile you were demonstrating."

Tony's head swam with the effort of remaining upright, but he remembered the correct response.

"I refuse."

Instantly Yinsen whirled on him, eyes blazing, and backhanded Tony across the face. "You *refuse?* You will do everything he says! This is the great Abu Bakar. You're alive only because of his generosity. You are nothing. *Nothing!* He offers you his hospitality, and you answer only with insolence! He will not be refused. You will die in a pool of your own blood!"

The leader, Abu Bakar, obviously understood English much better than he spoke it. He ate Yinsen's speech up, standing straighter and practically glowing with smug satisfaction.

With a glare at Tony, Abu turned and headed out of the cave, his henchmen following him. They slammed the door shut and locked it.

Yinsen waited to make sure they weren't coming back, then faced Tony, all the sudden rage gone in a heartbeat. "Perfect. You did very well, Stark."

Tony sat down on the edge of the couch, gray-faced and exhausted and perplexed as hell.

"I think they're starting to trust me," Yinsen said. He returned to the pot and started stirring it again. Almost cheerfully, he added, "Well, that's the end of *my* plan."

Tony stretched back out on the cot, wondering how he came to be surrounded by lunatics.

Chapter Six

Tony thought it was the next day, but he couldn't be sure. Things always looked the same inside the cave, and he'd been drifting in and out of sleep for a while . . . though he did at least feel as if he had some strength back.

He couldn't get used to the weight of the plate sutured into his chest. Almost as annoying as that was the need to carry the car battery around with him wherever he went.

Abu Bakar's men had come minutes before, and now prodded both Tony and Yinsen down the length of the cave's exit tunnel.

Tony stumbled along, a hood over his head, constantly getting jabbed in the back by Abu's henchmen. He could tell they were approaching the cave's entrance.

Then someone jerked the hood off his head, and Tony found himself standing in broad daylight, looking out into a camp set up in a small, bowl-shaped valley ringed by high, craggy mountains. Except it wasn't a camp, he realized with swiftly mounting shock, so much as a munitions dump.

Camouflage tarps had been rolled up, exposing skid after skid of Stark Industries weapons, countless rows of them lining the floor of the valley. Tony stared. Some of the crates dated back to the 1980s, relics of the Soviet invasion of Afghanistan. The Stark Industries munitions logo was faded and chipped. Others seemed to be brand-new, fresh off the assembly line.

Stunned, Tony staggered along one line of crates. He barely noticed Yinsen following along behind him.

"Quite a collection, isn't it?" Yinsen asked conversationally.

"How did they get all this?"

Abu, again flanked by his armed henchmen, moved closer to them and spoke. Yinsen paid attention and relayed Abu's words to Tony. "As you can see, they have everything you need to build the Jericho. He says to make a list of materials. You will start work right away, and when you are done he will set you free."

Tony scanned the whole camp. Only now could he start to see past the immense stores of weaponry and take note of the dozens of gun-toting Afghans all around them.

Off to one side was a tall, heavily armed, imposing man who stood and watched Tony, unblinking, his thick arms folded across his chest. A group of smaller men milled around him like pilot fish.

Softly, to Yinsen, Tony said, "No, he won't."

Yinsen hesitated, then whispered, "No. He won't."

At that moment, back at the site where Abu Bakar's fighters had ambushed the Humvee convoy, Rhodey grimly surveyed the cold, charred wreckage. Next to him stood General Benson Gabriel, a severe-looking man in his fifties. More of the Air Force security detail combed the area around them.

Rhodey scowled at the mangled Humvees. "Something's not right."

"Looks like a standard hit-and-run," Gabriel said. He sounded skeptical.

"Sir, I'm telling you, this was a snatch-and-grab. A perfectly executed linear ambush. As soon as they got what they wanted, they melted away."

The general lit a cigarette. "Intel's on it, we're in good hands. If he's out there, we'll get him."

An unpleasant mountain-born wind glided past them and died down before Rhodey spoke again. "With your permission I'd like to stay in-theater and head up the search and investigation."

General Gabriel flicked ashes off the end of his cigarette. "There's a PR firestorm brewing over this. Right now the best way to serve your country is to get back there and handle it."

Rhodey persisted. "Tony Stark is the DOD's number one intellectual asset, and I can be of value in the field."

"Duly noted, but we need you back home." Gabriel

threw down his cigarette, ground it out with the heel of his boot, and turned to walk back to his own Humvee. He paused after a few steps, but didn't look back as he spoke to Rhodey. "Lieutenant Colonel, it's not lost on me that Stark is a lifelong friend."

Rhodey nodded, hating the decision but abiding by it. He fell in line behind the general.

Hours stretched into . . . what? Days? Weeks? It was impossible to tell inside the cave.

Tony Stark sat in a wheelbarrow next to the furnace, the flames of which provided the only source of light in his "laboratory." He stared into space, an army surplus blanket wrapped around him, and pointedly ignored Yinsen, who stood nearby.

The car battery sat on the ground next to the wheelbarrow.

"I'm sure your people are looking for you," Yinsen said, "but they will never find you here." He got no response from Tony. He tried a different tack. "That battery is running out . . . and they won't turn on the generator till you start working."

Nothing. No response. Not even a blink.

Tony sat as if frozen solid.

"You didn't like what you saw when they took us out into the camp, did you? I didn't like it either when those weapons destroyed my village."

Yinsen tried to move into Tony's line of sight, but it was as though Tony were staring straight through him. "What you just saw, that's your legacy—your life's work in the hands of these murderers. Is that how you want to go out? Is this the last act of defiance of the great Tony Stark? Or are you going to try to do something about it?"

Finally Tony spoke, his voice dull and flat. "Why should I do anything? They're either going to kill me or I'm going to die in a week."

Yinsen folded his arms. "Then this is a very important week for you."

Tony didn't answer.

His father's face hung in the air in front of him, as solid and real as it ever had been when Howard Stark was alive. Tony could look his father straight in the eye, but he was ashamed to do it.

That stockpile of munitions had shaken Tony's world down to its core.

I value the weapons you only have to use once, he had said on many occasions, paraphrasing his father. Howard Stark always had a saying or a platitude of some kind ready to go, some cliché to fit whatever circumstance came up. From anyone else they would have sounded forced and trite, but Tony's father had a way of infusing practically any group of words or sentences with a sage wisdom, so that even something as dusty as "Good fences make good neighbors" suddenly became worthy of note.

"I value the weapon you only have to use once" took its place in the Howard Stark Hall of Wisdom alongside "peace means having a bigger stick than the other guy." Except now Tony couldn't help but think that these cave-dwelling, terrorist insurgents were the ones with the bigger stick.

And somehow, someway, Tony was the one who'd given it to them. The wrenching guilt hurt worse than any kind of physical chest wound.

How could this have happened? Stark Industries weapons were supposed to be used for surgical strikes, not carpet-bombings. Stark Industries weapons were the tools of choice of master tacticians and strategists. They were designed to find the weak point in whatever obstacle they faced—whether that was the fuel tank in an enemy fighter jet or the remote hideout of a guerrilla warlord—and eliminate that threat with extreme prejudice and pinpoint accuracy.

One Jericho missile could vaporize this entire camp, Tony thought morosely. *And me along with it. Maybe I should build what Abu Bakar wants me to. Maybe it'd be best if Tony Stark and all his misplaced toys out there simply ceased to be.*

But he knew, as appalling as the contraband munitions stockpile was, it was almost certainly not the only one of its kind. Even if there were no more Stark Industries ammo dumps out there, the black market made sure that men like Abu Bakar would never run short of weapons.

It just stung especially sharply that it was *his* weaponry they'd gotten their hands on.

Again, the questions came to him: *How? What do I do?*

One of the sayings the senior Stark had been most

57

fond of floated up from the depths of Tony's memory: "Necessity is the mother of invention."

Well, I've got one hell of a necessity, Tony said to himself. *So maybe it's time to start inventing.*

Slowly, laboriously, Tony unfolded his cramping legs and climbed out of the wheelbarrow. Yinsen raised curious eyebrows at him, and Tony said, "I need something to write on."

The clanking, whirring sound of an ancient generator starting up filled the cave seconds before all the lights came on. Abu Bakar and his two cronies—Yinsen had told Tony their names were Ahmed and Omar—stood watching him, flanked by several more armed guards.

Tony and Yinsen watched as Omar tipped a gas can into the generator, filling it, before returning the can to a security cage that also held a large fuel drum. Omar locked the cage and moved back to Abu's side.

Tony took that as his cue and began pacing as he barked out his demands. "Okay, here's what I need." Yinsen rapidly translated into Dari. "S-Category missiles. Lot 7043. The S-30 explosive tritonal. And a dozen of the S-76. Mortars: M-Category numbers one, four, eight, twenty, and sixty. M-229's: I need eleven of these. Mines: the pre-90's AP5's and AP16's."

Abu's men had started bringing in missiles and material to the cage while Tony talked. One of them frantically scribbled notes on a filthy notepad, and when Tony paused for breath, ripped off the top sheet and handed it to a runner. The men darted about, moving things, making room for everything Tony had requested.

Tony continued. "I need this area free of clutter, with good light. I want it at twelve o'clock to the door to avoid logjams. I need welding gear—either acetylene or propane, helmets, a soldering setup with goggles, and smelting cups. Two full sets of precision tools."

Yinsen dutifully translated. Abu grew visibly more exasperated with each item Tony called out.

"Finally, I want three pairs of white tube socks, a toothbrush, protein powder, spices, sugar, five pounds of tea, some playing cards . . ." He paused, thinking, either missing or deliberately ignoring Abu's widening eyes and throbbing forehead veins. ". . . and a washing machine. Top load."

Abu raged forward and got right in Tony's face. In Dari, he shouted, *"A washing machine? Does he think I'm a fool?"*

As calmly as if he were ordering a drink at an upscale bar, and without flinching, Tony said to Abu, "Must have everything. Great Satan make big boom— kill for powerful Abu Bakar. Big boom kill."

Breathing hard, Abu turned on his heel and stormed out.

Tony shot a glance at Yinsen and was pleased to see the older man doing his best to stifle laughter.

Chapter Seven

By the next day Abu Bakar had not returned to the cave to kill either of them, so Tony decided it was safe to begin work. After he and Yinsen shared a meager breakfast, he opened up a missile housing, carefully reached inside, and pulled out a small glass ring.

Yinsen watched. Tony set the glass ring aside, beckoned to Yinsen, and led him over to a large missile crate. "Can you give me a hand with this?"

"Of course. What am I giving you a hand *with*?"

"I'll explain as we go."

Working together, the two of them opened the crate, disassembled part of the housing on a larger missile, and removed the chip-rack cylinder from the warhead.

Yinsen said, "You *do* know they removed all the explosives before they brought this to us."

Tony lifted the heavy chip-rack. "I know. They're crazy, not stupid." Straining and grunting, he walked the chip-rack over to his newly placed workbench, set it down carefully, and used a pair of needle-nose pliers to remove a small strip of metal from inside the cylinder.

Yinsen raised an eyebrow. Tony held up the strip and said, "Palladium. This is what we're looking for. I need eleven of these."

"Eleven? For what purpose?"

Tony let the ghost of a smile touch his lips. "Just help me gather them. And I'm afraid you'll have to do the heavy lifting. If I lift one more of these things I'm afraid I'll rupture myself."

Tony and Yinsen spent the next couple of hours harvesting palladium strips. Yinsen located the chip-racks and brought them to Tony, who removed the strips and set them carefully aside. When they had enough, Tony asked Yinsen to heat up the furnace again.

Tony brought the metal strips over once the blaze was roaring. "Heat the palladium to 1828 Kelvin."

Standing next to the furnace, his face red and sweating from the heat, Yinsen asked, "How will I know when it reaches that temperature?"

"The palladium will melt."

"Fair enough. I have to say, Stark, this *really* doesn't look to me as though you're preparing to build a missile."

Tony regarded him blandly. "Oh, no? What does it look like to you?"

Yinsen shrugged. "I can't tell. It just doesn't look like a missile."

Tony made a small, noncommittal sound and, to Yinsen's visible frustration, ambled off to work on something else.

The rest of the afternoon disappeared in a haze of heat and molten metal. Yinsen didn't understand what Tony Stark was doing, but Tony seemed quite determined and perfectly confident, so he followed the younger man's instructions.

Yinsen observed carefully as Tony wrapped a copper coil around the glass ring he had taken from the smaller missile housing. They had set up a makeshift crucible on top of the furnace, into which they dropped the palladium strips; then, while the strips heated and began to melt, Tony sculpted a sand mold on the workbench.

The two men waited patiently for the palladium to reach its melting point. "You know we're witnessing a miracle here," Yinsen said conversationally.

"How so?"

"It's a miracle the furnace itself hasn't melted."

Tony gave Yinsen a weak clap on the back. "Have faith."

"Faith in what?"

Tony peered into the crucible, and by way of answering, said, "Okay, bring this over to the sand mold."

Yinsen carefully carried the crucible to the work-bench. Tony said, "Careful, careful . . ."

"Relax. I always have steady hands. It's why you're still alive."

"Oh, yeah. Thanks."

They both watched pensively as the molten metal filled the mold.

After the palladium had cooled and solidified into a ring, Tony carefully lifted it out of the mold with a tweezer and held it up appraisingly.

Yinsen stared at the ring for a few seconds, then glanced around at all the munitions in the lab. More matter-of-factly now, he asked, "What are you building?"

His tone cryptic, Tony answered, "A better mouse-trap."

Once again Tony felt the strange disconnect from the passage of time. He knew it had been days, but he wasn't sure how many, and he was irritated at himself for not keeping closer track. The work had simply taken up all his thoughts.

One morning—he felt pretty sure it was morning anyway—as Tony plugged a cable into the generator, he looked over and saw Yinsen shaving.

Tony stood up. "What are you shaving for? We're almost done."

Yinsen didn't answer for a few seconds, taking his time along his jawline. "Look like an animal, and soon you'll start behaving like one."

Tony threw a switch on the generator. The lights in the cave wavered, dimmed, then came back on. He moved to the side, so that both he and Yinsen could see what he had spent so much time on.

Resting on the workbench was a small, odd-looking device: a metallic disk, not much bigger than a coaster, ringed with softly glowing blue lights. The cable Tony had plugged into the generator ran across the floor, up onto the bench, and was attached to the disk.

As they watched, the blue lights began to glow more brightly.

Yinsen finished shaving, set down his razor, and wandered over to stand beside Tony, both of them looking down at the disk. Tony waited until the blue lights had achieved a steady glow. Then he disconnected the cable and held the disk up.

"That doesn't look like a Jericho missile," Yinsen said dryly.

"It is and it isn't," Tony replied. "This is a Repulsor device. A miniature ARK Reactor. The Jericho uses the same technology, but in a much more explosive fashion. *This* is a power converter and accumulator. Once it's charged, as it is now, it should suspend the shrapnel in my chest and keep it from entering my heart."

Some of the technical information was lost on Yinsen, but he grasped the larger concepts with no trouble. Dryly, he said, "What an original invention."

"Yeah, but this one is going to last a bit longer than a week."

Yinsen's forehead wrinkled. "It's pretty small. What can it generate?"

"Three gigajoules. *Per second.*"

That registered. Yinsen's eyes bugged and his jaw dropped open. "But . . . that . . . that could run your heart for fifty lifetimes!"

"Or something very big for fifteen minutes."

Their eyes met, understanding flashing back and forth between them. Tony said, "Let's put it in."

At that moment, in a small control room elsewhere in the camp, the tall, imposing man who had watched Tony with a baleful eye at the munitions dump sat and stared at a monitor. His name was Raza, and everything about him, from the set of his jaw to the cruel line of his mouth, to the huge, chiseled muscles of his body, screamed *danger*. He gave off the air of a coiled, venomous snake, unpredictable and lethal.

On the monitor, Tony Stark lay on the workbench in the cave, with Yinsen leaning over him.

Raza held a large metal can of U.S. military-issue peanut butter. He spooned huge gobbets of it into his mouth, eating slowly, deliberately. But he never took his eyes off the screen, and he never blinked.

• • •

As he worked, Yinsen said to Tony, "I don't understand. This Repulsor Technology—this is something you invented?"

"After a fashion. I stood on the shoulders of giants, as the saying goes. In this case, the giant was my father."

"But . . . but power can neither be created nor destroyed," Yinsen said. "It's a basic law of the universe. You hook up this tiny thing to the generator for five minutes, and now suddenly it can give you all this power, over so long a time? How is that possible?"

Tony gladly settled into explanatory mode, since it took his mind off what Yinsen was currently doing to him. "It's a matter of efficiency. Every energy source we've got, from the internal combustion engine to the most powerful nuclear power plant, all of them are, to put it in layman's terms, horribly inefficient. Only a tiny percentage of the power generated is actually usable."

"All right," Yinsen said. "You've got me hooked. And you can keep talking, if you can do that while holding very still. At this point in the process, you don't want to make any sudden movements."

"You know, your bedside manner is really atrocious."

Yinsen said, "Less criticism, more holding still."

Tony sighed. "Well, there's not much more to it, really. This little glowy thing we've put together? It's an accumulator . . . and it's about ninety-eight percent efficient. Nobody's ever done that before. Ever. Repulsor Technology has finally broken through the efficiency barrier. That little disk can do what it does because it takes the electricity I feed into it, processes it, and releases it at roughly 98.99% efficiency. To put it very crudely, it gives you way more bang for the buck than anything else on the planet."

"Stark . . . what you're describing to me . . . it sounds too good to be true." Yinsen paused in his activity, brow furrowing. "Why hasn't this been released to the world?" A dark thought suddenly occurred to him. "Stark, why are you using this mirac-ulous thing only in *weapons?*"

Tony closed his eyes. "This disk you're about to implant in my chest? Do you remember how many missiles we had to disassemble to get the necessary components?"

Yinsen thought about it. "Fifteen?"

"Seventeen. Seventeen missiles, each of which has a price tag in excess of one-point-five million dollars U.S."

"Oh . . . so you're saying . . ."

"I'm saying the average American consumer doesn't have twenty-six million dollars just lying around."

Yinsen stayed quiet for a while, working and think-ing about what Tony had said. "So . . . this thing you created . . . correct me if I'm wrong, please. But it sounds as if you've invented something whose only practical application—as wondrous as the device itself may be—is as the kind of weapon that only the military could possibly afford."

"Well, hey," Tony said bleakly, no joy in his voice, "I *am* a weapons manufacturer."

Neither of them spoke again until Yinsen had completed his work.

Chapter Eight

Half a world away, the Los Angeles sunlight shone through the enormous windows in the hallway leading to Tony Stark's office. The light glinted beautifully off Pepper Potts's hair, but Pepper's face betrayed no emotion as she walked with a purposeful stride.

She carried two carefully folded newspapers: the *L.A. Times* and the *Wall Street Journal*. As she reached the door to Tony's office, she unconsciously smoothed her hair, even though not a strand was out of place.

Pepper stopped in the doorway, surprised to see Obadiah Stane sitting at Tony's desk, his head in his hands in a classic pose of worry and anxiety.

Obadiah looked up, instantly apologetic. "Sorry, did I startle you?"

"A little," Pepper said, calm again. Obadiah watched as she came to the desk and replaced yesterday's editions of Tony's favorite newspapers with today's.

None of them had been read.

Obadiah stood and gazed out the window. From there he had the same view that Tony always had: the vast Stark Industries compound, with the futuristic ARK Reactor building at the far end, its ultramodern architecture a herald of things to come.

Just beyond the Reactor, the grounds sloped sharply, ending at one of L.A.'s bustling freeways. Motorists on the freeway could look up and see the Reactor, poised above them, a symbol not only of the future, but also of Stark Industries' presence.

Pepper came up behind Obadiah, quietly taking in the view herself.

"This was a bad idea," he said, guilt in his voice. "I should never have let him go over there."

Obadiah's refined, dignified face began to quiver, and tears filled his eyes. Pepper touched his shoulder.

"Hey, hey . . ." she said softly. "We've got to be strong. He's going to be okay."

With some effort, Obadiah composed himself and nodded.

The two of them stayed there for a while longer, gazing out over the life's work of their missing friend.

Tony Stark finally began marking down each day as it passed, but soon wished he hadn't bothered. Days became weeks, and weeks soon threatened to become months, and still he hadn't left the cave.

But then, he hadn't stopped working, either.

The cave's interior looked significantly different now. The missiles and other materials had all been moved, disassembled, and scavenged, and now a huge metal framework stood in the center of the "lab" area, a jig designed to hold the missile's components in place as Tony welded, bolted, and soldered them together.

The car battery lay off to one side, carelessly tossed against a wall. Its leads still ran to the bulky chestplate, which also lay in the dirt, the blood around its edges old and dried.

Standing at an anvil, Tony Stark used an acetylene torch to cut a flat, gray piece of metal. He sported a full beard now, his color and strength obviously improved as well—and his shirt lay open, exposing the glowing Repulsor unit now implanted in his chest.

Beyond him, Yinsen sat at a smaller workbench, carefully putting together a backgammon board. The older man's personal grooming habits hadn't changed. He was just as closely shaven as he had always been.

Tony glanced around and saw that Yinsen was intent on his project. Using his own body to block Yinsen's view, Tony began surreptitiously filling a small metal cylinder with acetylene from the cutting torch.

Yinsen didn't even look in Tony's direction. "Stark, you tell me what you're doing, and I'll tell you what I'm doing."

Tony kept his back to Yinsen and continued filling the cylinder. It was a slow process. "Looks to me like you're making a crappy backgammon board."

"Crappy? This is Lebanese cedar."

"Is that where you're from? Lebanon?"

"I'm impressed that you even know what this is." Yinsen sat back and looked at Tony. "How about we play, and if I win, you tell me what you're really making."

"A: I don't know what you're talking about. B: I was the backgammon champ at MIT four years running."

Yinsen gave Tony a tiny smile with a challenge behind it. "Interesting. I was the champion at Cambridge."

Tony warmed to the thought of some verbal sparring. "Please don't use 'interesting' and 'Cambridge' in the same sentence. Is that even still a school?"

"It's a university. You probably haven't heard about it since Americans can't get in."

"Unless they're teaching."

Before Yinsen could respond, the door flew open and Abu Bakar stormed in, barking orders in Dari. Startled, Tony dropped the cylinder, which clattered to the floor.

Yinsen saw the cylinder and shot Tony a pointed look.

Abu and his henchmen, Ahmed and Omar, entered the cave and stepped to the side, making way for a new group of men: the guards Tony had seen milling around Raza outside in the camp. They in turn stepped aside, and Raza himself entered.

In English, Raza said, "My name is Raza. The two of you can relax."

Tony and Yinsen exchanged glances. Neither of them had dealt with this man before, and weren't sure whether or not to take him at his word. But he seemed to be genuine, and they slowly, carefully let their hands drop.

No one spoke as Raza began meandering around the lab, picking things up, putting them back down. Tony stopped breathing for a second as Raza almost stepped on the gas-filled cylinder, but then Raza spotted the washing machine and shot Abu Bakar a cold, deadly look.

The big man kept his composure, though, as he drifted over to the workbench and perused Tony's onion-paper schematics for the Jericho missile.

Raza spoke in a low voice. "The bow and arrow was once the pinnacle of weapons technology. It allowed the great Genghis Khan to rule from the Pacific to the Ukraine." He shuffled the schematics around. Though this was clearly a dangerous man, Tony noted that Raza didn't seem to understand engineering at all. "Today . . . whoever has the latest Stark weapons rules these lands. Soon it will be my turn . . ."

Raza looked back and forth between Tony and Yinsen, then spoke to Yinsen in Urdu. *"What's really going on here?"*

Yinsen answered him, also in Urdu: *"Nothing. We're working."*

"It's been a long time. Where's the weapon?"

Yinsen gestured to the jig and the surrounding components. *"He's working very hard. It's very complex."*

Tony strained to interpret the scene, trying to read the men's body language.

To Abu, still in Urdu, Raza said, *"Get him on his knees."*

Abu scurried forward with Omar and Ahmed, pointing and barking orders. The two henchmen grabbed Yinsen and forced him to his knees. Tony lifted a hand, about to say something, but Omar shoved his gun in Tony's face.

Tony remained still, gritting his teeth, the muscles in his jaw rippling.

Moving slowly, Raza picked up a pair of tongs, opened the door to the furnace, and removed a glowing red coal. He turned, eyeing Yinsen, and moved toward him, still very slowly. In Urdu, he asked, *"Tell me what is going on."*

Yinsen couldn't take his eyes off the coal. *"Nothing! Nothing is going on!"*

Raza shot his head forward like a striking cobra and roared in Yinsen's face, *"Open your mouth!"*

Yinsen shivered, staring at the coal, but his eyebrows drew together, and through his trembling he shook his head. Raza snarled and motioned to Omar and Ahmed, who immediately grabbed Yinsen's head and brutally forced his mouth open.

The coal hovered close enough to burn Yinsen's lips. Tony watched, helpless and furious, as Raza screamed again, *"Tell me now!"*

Trembling, miserable, Yinsen whispered, *"He's building your bomb."*

74

The coal moved closer to Yinsen's open mouth . . . closer . . . and Raza dropped the coal on the floor in front of Yinsen, turned on his heel, and walked out of the cave as if both Yinsen and Tony had abruptly ceased to exist. Omar and Ahmed released Yinsen and trailed after Abu as everyone left the cave.

Yinsen almost collapsed. Tony rushed to him, supporting him. Yinsen panted for a few seconds, then stood, collected himself, and brushed off his clothing.

"That's *twice* I've saved your life," he said tightly. "Now are you going to tell me what the hell you're really building?"

Tony met Yinsen's eyes and came to a decision. He led Yinsen to a light-board on his workbench and flicked it on. Wordlessly Tony pulled a completely separate stack of onionskin schematics out from under a pile of scrap metal pieces and laid them on the board.

Surprise shifted to gradual understanding on Yinsen's face as Tony let the schematics do the talking for him.

"Finally," Yinsen said, as a new note of respect found its way into his words. "An idea all your own."

Another day came and went, marked only by Abu Bakar's attempt to catch Tony Stark in some sort of underhanded act by suddenly throwing open the door slat and peering in at them.

He only saw Tony shaving. The door slat slammed, and they heard Abu's footsteps fade as he stomped away.

75

Tony finished shaving, toweled off his face, and pulled on a pair of heavy work gloves as he went to the furnace. Using the same pair of tongs Raza had used to threaten Yinsen, Tony took a piece of white-hot metal from the furnace, carried it to the anvil nearby, and began pounding on it with a hammer.

Yinsen, busy soldering a complex circuit, looked up at the first swing of the hammer and was struck by the sight of Tony, strong and resolute, pounding out the metal.

Suddenly Yinsen remembered a childhood story his grandfather had told him.

My people have a tale about a prince—much hated by his king—who was banished to the underworld and jailed there.

The hammer blows echoed around the cave, growing louder and louder, like cannon shots.

The evil king gave the prince the most difficult labor: working the iron pits.

Tony grunted with effort, the muscles in his arms and shoulders flexing, sweat flying off of him as he worked.

Year after year the prince mined the heavy ore, becoming so strong he could crush pieces of it together with his bare hands. Too late the king realized his mistake.

A hammer blow sprayed a dazzling shower of sparks around Tony.

When the king struck at the prince with his finest sword, the blade broke in half. The prince himself had become as strong as iron.

Tony held up the piece of metal he'd been working

on and Yinsen gasped involuntarily as a crude iron mask stared back at Tony. He tossed the mask down, and it lay there, smoking and pulsing with heat.

Under his breath, Yinsen whispered two words, charged with the power of myth and strength and revolution.

"Iron Man."

Chapter Nine

A rare afternoon thundershower pelted the Stark Industries headquarters as Pepper Potts made her way down one of the broad corridors. She turned a corner and stopped, halted by the scene playing out in front of her.

At the far end of the hallway near the main entrance stood Obadiah Stane and Rhodey, deep in conversation. The talk came to an end as she watched. Obadiah, his expression grave, glanced over and caught Pepper's eye, then turned and walked away from Rhodey, shaking his head disgustedly.

Pepper knew in an instant what the conversation meant.

Rhodey headed for the door, but she caught up to him before he made it out of the building. "So that's it?" she demanded. "Everyone's pulling the plug and moving on?"

"There's nothing left we can do. If there were any indication Tony was still alive . . ." He trailed off. The sadness in Rhodey's voice was not lost on Pepper, but she didn't care.

"Spare me. I read the official email. Thought maybe you'd have something different to say."

He glanced around. "Could we not do this here?"

"Fine. Come with me."

Rhodey followed Pepper to her office, where she picked up the thread as soon as the door closed. "If anyone could figure out how to beat the odds, it's Tony. If it was you over there, he'd be finding a way to get you back. Or inventing a new one."

"Pepper . . . Pepper, look, I'm doing what I can, all right?"

She paused at an undefinable note in his voice. "What do you mean, what you can?"

"I mean exactly what I said." Rhodey turned to go, but stopped with his hand on the door. "He's my friend. It's not like I haven't been taking steps. I just wish they could be *bigger* steps."

Rhodey opened the door and walked out, leaving Pepper standing there feeling a tiny shred of newfound hope.

Early the next morning at Edwards Air Force Base, Lieutenant Colonel James Rhodes stood in a line of other soldiers, duffel slung across his back, waiting to board a C-17 transport plane. He glanced around at the faint sound of an electric motor approaching, and saw General Gabriel barreling toward him in a golf cart.

Everyone snapped perfect salutes as the general got out of the cart and pulled Rhodey aside.

"What do you think you're doing, Rhodes?"

Rhodey didn't bat an eye. "Going back there, sir."

Gabriel scowled. "Listen, son——it's been three months without a single indication that Stark is still alive. We can't keep risking assets, least of all you."

"Are you blocking my transfer, sir?"

The general glanced around at the other soldiers, all of them still standing at rigid attention. "Any one of these guys would kill for your career. Are you telling me you're willing to sacrifice that to fly a bunch of snake-eaters on a desert patrol halfway around the world?"

Without hesitation, Rhodey answered: "I am, sir."

"Then I have one thing to say to you," Gabriel growled. "Godspeed."

The general saluted Rhodey, who immediately returned it. To the other men, the general said, "As you were."

Rhodey nodded gratefully at General Gabriel, turned, and headed up the loading ramp with the rest of the soldiers.

As closely as he could figure it, Tony Stark had been in the cave for four months, two weeks, and five days. If he had been trapped here with nothing to do, he felt quite confident that he would have gone irreversibly insane.

But he had given himself things to do. *Plenty* of

them. And they all led to this.

Shortly after the evening meal, Tony put the finishing touches on a small, odd-looking box. Inside the box, mounted on a tiny but sturdily built framework, was a fan, a cluster of tinsel, and a laser pointer. Tony carefully taped the box shut, lifted it to eye level, and peered through a pinhole in its side.

To Tony's eye, the interior of the box looked just like the furnace's flames in the dark.

"Perfect," he whispered.

In Raza's control room, guards milled about, bored and unconcerned with keeping a close eye on the monitors.

Consequently, no one noticed when one of the monitors—the one focused on the blaze in the furnace—went dark for a split second, then resumed its surveillance.

In the cave lab, Tony stepped back from the security camera lens to which he had just affixed the pinhole box. Wasting no time, Tony moved to the workbench and snapped on a small but high-powered light. Yinsen was waiting for him.

"You ready?"

Yinsen nodded. "Eager, even."

"Then let's get going."

The two men worked in relative silence for several long minutes. When they were finished, a motion sensor was attached to Tony's leg and, suspended from the

81

assembly jig, a vertical contraption of rods and cylinders hung motionless. Waiting.

Tony took a wire running from the sensor and plugged it into his Repulsor "heart." On the workbench, a crusty, outdated laptop computer lit up with data racing onto its screen.

Tony took a deep breath. "Here goes nothing," he murmured, and raised his leg. Immediately, and in perfect sync, the contraption on the jig sprang to life and mimicked his leg's motion. The blue lights on the Repulsor unit dimmed with the power loss.

They were quiet about it, but when Tony and Yinsen looked each other in the eye, the triumph practically filled the cave.

Tony unplugged himself. "We're ready. A week of assembly and we're a go."

Yinsen nodded. "Then perhaps it's time we settle another matter."

Tony understood what he meant and broke out into a rakish grin, but it wasn't until the next day that they found time to sit down and address Yinsen's concern: a good, solid game of backgammon.

The two men sat across from each other, the game between them atop a discarded cable spool set on end. Both of them stared at the board and only at the board, playing as if wagers of incalculable value had been made.

With quiet respect, Yinsen said, "Ah, anchoring with the 13-7. You know, I have never met anyone who understands the nuances of this game as well as you do."

"Right back at ya." Tony paused. "You never told me where you're from."

When Yinsen spoke, the lighthearted competitive air had disappeared. His voice was thick with controlled but deeply felt emotion. "I come from a small village not far from here. It was a good place . . . before these men ravaged it."

"Do you have a family?"

The older man nodded. "When I get out of here, I am going to see them again. Do you have family, Stark?"

It was Tony's turn to hesitate. Finally he said, "No."

"You're a man who has everything and nothing."

Tony considered that. He started to say, "I don't have *nothing*," thinking about Pepper and Rhodey and Obadiah.

But what were they to him? More to the point, how did he *treat* them? Did he behave as if Rhodey were a trusted, loyal friend? As if Pepper were an indispensable and brilliant colleague? As if Obadiah were a patient, wise father figure whom Tony could lean on?

When was the last time he'd leaned on anyone? Tony Stark didn't lean, he realized. Tony Stark *pushed*. Tony's face clouded as he turned that unpleasant truth over in his mind.

Suddenly the door opened and Abu stomped into the cave.

In Dari, and without looking up from the game, Yinsen said, *"Your laundry's over there."*

Abu crossed the cave to a basket on the workbench,

filled with laundered and neatly folded clothes. He picked it up and took a deep breath, with a look on his face that seemed to say, 'Ah, clean clothes.' Then he headed back for the door, carrying the basket, and shook his head when he looked over and saw they were playing backgammon.

Still in Dari, Abu said, "*You idiots don't know what you're doing with that game.*"

Impatiently and dismissively, Tony said, "Yeah, yeah, enjoy your laundry."

Abu smirked and took another step, and then froze solid when Raza stepped through the door into the cave.

Sensing the sudden tension in the chamber, both Tony and Yinsen looked up, and so both of them witnessed Raza's gaze travel from Abu's face down to the laundry basket.

Raza's eyes seemed to freeze over with an icy crust of hatred.

With no further warning, Raza drew a pistol and shot Abu Bakar through the forehead. The laundry crashed to the floor. Abu's body followed it half a second later.

Neither Tony nor Yinsen moved a muscle.

As Raza's guards came in to dispose of Abu's body, Raza turned eyes as black as ink and as deadly as a pit viper's on Tony. "You have till tomorrow to assemble my missile," he said in English, his voice echoing around the cave.

Then he turned and walked out, letting a deep and profound silence fall in his wake.

● ● ●

The following day, in Raza's control room, a young man named Khalid sat and stared at the monitors, alert and watchful. Behind him, some of Raza's henchmen pored over a map, heatedly discussing tactics while others cleaned and reassembled weapons.

On the central monitor, Yinsen was partially visible behind the assembly jig, furiously working on something out of sight. He kept making the same motion, over and over, as if he were cutting metal with a hacksaw.

Raza entered, moving silently and with surprising grace for a man of his size. He drifted over to the monitors, observing. He leaned in close, his hawk-sharp eyes fixed on the central monitor. The small, grainy image of Yinsen still flailed away behind the jig.

Raza spoke in Urdu, his voice tight: *"Khalid. Where is Stark?"*

Less than a minute later, Khalid and several armed guards sprinted down the tunnel to the cave lab. They arrived at the door and Khalid slammed the door slat aside to peer in. What he could see greatly resembled the view on the monitor: Yinsen, still behind the jig, still working furiously on something he couldn't make out.

"Yinsen!" Khalid shouted. *"Yinsen!"*

The older man ignored him and kept working.

Khalid tried the door and discovered it had been jammed shut, blocked from the other side.

Khalid was in no hurry to return to Raza and

explain that he still didn't know where Stark was because the old man wouldn't unlock the door. Glancing around at the men who had come with him, Khalid gestured at the door and mimed striking it with his rifle butt. The other men understood and nodded, giving him space.

What Khalid had no way of knowing was that the cylinder Tony had filled with acetylene gas was rigged to the door's latch. He tried once more to open the door, verified that it still wouldn't budge, and then threw all of his weight against it, shoulder-first.

An ear-splitting explosion blasted Khalid backward and filled the tunnel with smoke and debris.

Chapter Ten

On the workbench in the cave, barely visible through the smoke from the explosion, program bars crept across the screen of the decrepit laptop.

"It's frozen, the systems aren't talking to each other. Reset!"

Tony's voice came from behind the assembly jig, where Yinsen had been laboring.

"No," Yinsen answered. "They're moving. Very slow." He grunted, shifting a bulky piece of gunmetal-gray plating, and began lowering it over Tony Stark's chest, as Tony lay prone behind the jig. Once the piece was settled, Yinsen grabbed a pneumatic wrench and sealed it in place.

Raza hadn't moved from his place in the control room, where he had witnessed the explosion in the tunnel over a surveillance camera. He shouted orders over the radio, orchestrating his men; a dozen heavily armed fighters now made their way down the tunnel, rapidly approaching the cave lab.

In the lab, Yinsen eyed the laptop anxiously, watching the program bars creep slowly, so slowly, across the screen. The sounds of Raza's men outside grew steadily louder.

Tony's voice reached him. "Get to your cover. Remember the checkpoints. Make sure each one is clear before you follow me out."

Tony felt pretty good about the strategy they had worked out. It was extremely simple, but should be effective, and should also accomplish Tony's primary goal: getting himself and Yinsen out of here alive.

Tony realized something had gone wrong the moment he saw Yinsen's expression change. Yinsen closed his eyes for a moment, his hands clenching into fists and unclenching. He stared around the cave . . . and then he turned and sprinted out the door, straight toward Raza's men.

Tony screamed, *"Yinsen!"*

But the older man didn't stop. He passed through the ruined doorway, stepped over Khalid's blasted body, and picked up the dead man's gun. Then he bolted away from the lab, shouting and firing the rifle into the tunnel's ceiling.

He sounded like a whole squad of men, and when he rounded a corner and ran into Raza's fighters, they hesitated for a split second. It was enough to gain the upper hand, and Yinsen opened fire on them, screaming at the top of his lungs.

Raza's men broke and ran, panicked, many of them wounded and a couple already dead.

Yinsen continued his charge, chasing the men all the way to the tunnel's entrance, where it opened into a much larger cavern and where he suddenly found himself face-to-face with Raza and dozens more men, all with weapons trained on him.

Yinsen fell silent and slowly lowered his rifle to the ground.

Back inside the cave lab, Tony Stark lay still, encased in metal, unable to move. His eyes, trapped behind a metal mask, darted frantically from the laptop and its infuriatingly slow progress to the blasted door. The progress bars moved across the grimy screen, one tiny tick at a time, crawling from left to right. No, crawling was too generous a word, Tony decided. Tectonic plates moved faster than this.

From outside the lab came the sounds of multiple bursts of gunfire. This was followed seconds later by shouts and the running footsteps of . . . Tony couldn't even guess how many men. All of them getting closer—all of them coming to kill him.

And then the progress bars finished loading.

The computer gave out a tiny *ding* and a massive power surge dimmed the lights in the laboratory.

• • •

In the tunnel outside the lab, the lights flickered and dropped to complete darkness. Raza's guards, abruptly unnerved, slowed down and began inching toward the lab door. The two in front motioned to their comrades, then broke away and moved forward, weapons at the ready.

They entered the dark, smoke-filled lab, their eyes straining to see, their ears struggling to pick up any sounds of threat. The chamber appeared to be deserted. Then one of the men slowly turned to look behind him. There in the dark, obscured by smoke, was an eerie blue glow, hovering between two small jets of flame. The man tried to understand exactly what he was looking at, when suddenly the lab and tunnel both filled up with a horrible, screeching, surging noise as metal scraped across metal.

Both men screamed as a vast, awful strength hurled them out of the lab, back into the tunnel, straight into the waiting group of insurgents; the impact as the men slammed into their comrades was more than enough to break multiple bones.

Raza's guards shouted and opened fire into the lab, shooting blindly through the doorway, emptying their weapons into the mysterious smoke and gloom. They stopped to reload, scrambling to jam fresh magazines into their rifles.

In the silence they heard it: the thump of impossibly heavy footsteps. The screech and groan of metal. The men watched in terror as things emerged from the smoke: a glowing chest plate. Flickering blue pilot lights. Twin jets of flame.

A nightmare creature of gray metal stepped into the tunnel. Part armored knight, part science-fiction monster, the creature moved toward the insurgents one crunching footstep at a time.

The metal creature seemed to have constructed its body from scraps, taking whatever random pieces of metal it could find and grafting them to its skeleton. Black, empty eyes stared out from the domed head, set atop a wide, powerful body, its thick arms and legs substituting long strips of metal for muscles.

The men backpedaled, firing, but the creature wouldn't stop. The bullets ricocheted off its gray metal skin and didn't even slow it down.

From inside the gray armor—the armor he had spent the last four months building, the armor powered by the Repulsor unit grafted into his own chest—Tony Stark's lips curved into a grim smile. "Bring it on."

In his control room, Raza strapped on a flak jacket and grabbed a rocket-propelled grenade (RPG) launcher from a weapons rack in the corner. He ran back outside, back to the entrance to the tunnel, where his men were streaming inside, rushing to face the strange threat making its way toward the outside world.

Raza only had one frantic man's description of the thing coming toward them. He didn't truly believe the words spilling from the man's mouth, but he knew that, whatever it was, it had survived dozens of bullet wounds without falling.

Raza took an RPG from an ammo pouch around his waist and loaded the launcher.

In the exit tunnel, a brilliant streak of tracer bullets spiked through the darkness and slammed into Tony, their light-giving phosphorus exploding off his armor in a dazzling light-show. He squinted behind the mask and kept moving.

A screaming insurgent leaped out from a side tunnel, aimed a pistol squarely at the back of Tony's armored head, and pulled the trigger. The bullet ricocheted straight back with a *pinging* sound and killed the man instantly.

Tony kept going, one giant, heavy foot in front of the other, moving steadily toward the end of the tunnel and the light of freedom.

Suddenly, it was as if he'd kicked a beehive. Insurgents by the dozens sprang out of nooks and side tunnels, in front of him and behind him, all of them firing repeatedly.

Tony swung his arms, his armored fists like giant maces, and knocked several men senseless. But there were so many of them; too many to reach. They wouldn't stop shooting, even though the ricochets struck more of their own men than Tony's fists did. The barrage was too much. Nothing could stand up to that kind of punishment for that long.

The armor began to give way. Tiny cracks appeared, minuscule flakes of metal exploding off of it amid the countless pockmarks. Its joints began to smoke.

Gritting his teeth, Tony growled, "Time to speed this up."

In a nearby passageway, one that intersected the exit tunnel just before it reached the outer cavern, Raza walked very quickly, the RPG launcher ready in his hands. A wounded man reached up from the dirt floor and grabbed at him with bloody hands, but Raza kicked him violently aside.

His armor smoking, parts of it glowing with heat, and with practically every inch of it pockmarked with the impact of thousands of bullets, Tony Stark made his way out of the exit tunnel and into the larger cavern. Immediately, and to his horror, Tony spotted Yinsen, crumpled in a bloody heap on the ground a few yards in front of him.

Yinsen lifted his head and saw Tony. Then he saw something else and used his last ounce of strength to shout, "Stop! Stop!"

Tony froze in his tracks, just as a rocket-propelled grenade flashed past his face and exploded against a wall off to the side. Tony followed the grenade's flight path back to its origin, and saw Raza standing there calmly reloading an RPG launcher.

Tony turned to face Raza, his teeth grinding in fury, and raised his arms. Mounted on the backs of the armor's wrists, reinforced tubing connected to a heavily shielded tank built onto the suit's back. The tubes' nozzles were the sources of the twin flames the insurgents in the tunnel had seen, and Tony moved forward, readying the flamethrowers with Raza dead in his sights.

But the flames sputtered and died when he hit the activation switch inside his gauntlets.

"Oh, for the love of—come on, *come on*," Tony muttered, hitting the switch again and again.

Raza saw what was happening and immediately understood. He finished reloading the launcher and sauntered into the cavern, facing off against the man in the gray armor. "Looks as though you should have stuck to building missiles," he said in English, aiming the launcher. "Good-bye, Mr. Stark."

Tony hit the gauntlet switch one last time—and the dust of the earth itself scorched black as twin columns of fire erupted from the flamethrowers.

Raza flung the launcher to the side and flattened himself on the ground, but it was too little and too late. The fire enveloped him, and Raza screamed in agony before pulling one of his men on top of him as a shield.

Tony cleared the main cavern and the connecting tunnels of insurgents with long blasts of acetylene-powered flame, watching and listening as the last of the survivors ran away in mortal fear. Then he turned and moved back to Yinsen. The armor screeched and shrieked as he knelt beside the older man's bleeding body.

"I don't understand," Tony said, his voice catching.

"We could've made it. Both of us. You could've seen your family again!"

Yinsen's last breaths came in hitches. He had been trying to cover up the multiple bullet wounds in his chest, but now his hand fell away, and Tony almost cringed at the devastation. "Understanding . . . is . . . easy." Through the pain, a faraway smile flickered on Yinsen's lips. "I *am* going to . . . see them again. . . . They're waiting . . . for me."

The smile grew wider, brighter.

Then Yinsen's body sagged and he died.

Tony raised his head and stared at the exit of the cavern, the ragged-edged opening through which genuine sunlight could be seen. He stood, trembling, quaking with rage, the armor's metal gauntlets grinding into themselves with the force of his clenching fists.

Tony roared his anger and his grief, and as the sound emerged from the iron mask and echoed around the cavern, the man in the gray armor began to *run*.

Chapter Eleven

A scouring blast of flame jetted out from the cavern as Raza's remaining men screamed and ran, followed by the titanic, earth-rumbling footsteps of Tony Stark in his ragged gray armor.

Tony emerged into the daylight, the armor scarred and sizzling, and made his way unerringly toward the huge stockpile of Stark Industries weapons. The insurgents concentrated their fire on him, trying to draw him away, but though the armor was beginning to suffer, Tony didn't waver in his course.

When he got within range, Tony activated the flamethrowers again and sprayed fire over the closest of the munitions crates. The crates began to burn immediately. Tony watched in satisfaction as the Stark logos disappeared in blackened char.

But just then someone screamed an order, and the insurgents shot a barrage of gunfire so intense that it knocked Tony to his knees. One of the bullets nicked through the line to his right flamethrower. Flammable liquid sprayed all over his arm, which promptly caught fire while another bullet found its way through a newly burst seam and sank into Tony's shoulder. A strangled scream forced its way out of his throat.

But he got to his feet, more determined than ever. As the armor shrieked and ground in metallic protest, Tony forged ahead, entering the maze of aisles between the stacks of munitions crates. He used his one working flamethrower everywhere, torching everything in sight as he moved.

Finally Tony made it through to the other side of the stockpile. Rounds still pinged and ricocheted off of him, and pieces of the armor had begun to fall away, but a few of Raza's men seemed to have understood what the escalating blaze behind him meant. The number of bullet impacts grew fewer and farther between as the insurgents began running away, fleeing the encampment entirely.

"That's thing one," Tony whispered to himself, the tendons in his neck drawn tight with the pain from the bullet in his shoulder. "Time for thing two." He flipped open a panel on the back of his left forearm and hit a bright red switch.

A whine emanated from the armor. At first it was the sort of whine that might come from a small jet engine, but it quickly escalated, outpowering the roar of the fire behind him for sheer volume. Tony tucked down, angled forward, and the thrusters built into his heels flashed from red to yellow to white hot in seconds, kicking up plumes of dust fifty feet high or more. Suddenly Tony Stark blasted off like a missile, rising hundreds and hundreds of feet in the air.

On the ground below, Omar stood bloodied but alive. He watched, dumbstruck, as the man in the gray armor arced across the sky toward a distant mountain pass.

Then the first of the munitions crates detonated.

That explosion alone would have been enough to flatten the entire insurgents' camp; the surface-to-surface missiles inside that single crate were packed with high-yield explosives so powerful that one missile could easily destroy an entire apartment block.

Each crate in that stack held eight missiles.

And that initial detonation was only the first in a string of rapid-fire blasts, each one more powerful than the last as stack after stack went up and the shock waves fed on each other. The entire valley was demolished, scraped and scoured clean in an immense fireball that rivaled the blast of a hydrogen bomb. Riding high in the sky, Tony Stark watched in a combination of awe and sheer panic as the monstrous, all-consuming globe of flame kept expanding and came after him.

But Tony's boosters saved him, propelling him up and over the crest of one of the knifelike mountains, though only by inches. The inferno behind him slammed against the mountainside, licked it with tongues of searing flame, but didn't pass over the crest. Tony was safe.

And that's when his boosters ran out of fuel.

Suddenly a dead weight in the air, Tony plummeted

like a cannonball. He could do little more than watch through the eye-grilles of the armored mask as the ground came rushing up to meet him, a vast expanse of rock and sand dunes that seemed to stretch away forever.

Tony slammed into a dune on its far slope, rolling and crashing his way down, tumbling like a marionette with its strings suddenly cut. Pieces of the armor came loose and flew off him, littering the sand in his path with metallic gray debris.

Finally he came to rest at the bottom of the dune and lay there for a while without moving.

Silence broken only by the susurration of the desert wind descended around him. A tiny lizard scampered out from under a rock, inspected Tony's face, flicked its tongue out and tasted his skin, then retreated to its rock.

Tony's low shadow lengthened slightly.

When Tony at last gathered the energy to rise, he literally stood up out of the armor into which he had previously been sealed. There was nothing left . . . nothing but randomly scattered bits of junk.

Tony took a couple of staggering steps, his head filled with pain and disorienting flashes of light, and clutched his wounded, bleeding shoulder as he stumbled away among the dunes. He fell, crashing face-first into the sand, but slowly, doggedly got back up and kept moving.

Ignoring the trail of blood he was leaving in the sand, he staggered on relentlessly westward, one foot after the other.

• • •

Hours had passed. Tony knew that, because it was starting to get dark. Not much else registered in his brain at the moment, as he half-walked, half-fell down a steep dune.

He would have enjoyed the luxury of sunlight, denied him for so long in the dark, windowless cave lab, if he hadn't been so sure that he would die soon.

He was exhausted. He had no water. And the bullet hole in his shoulder wouldn't stop bleeding, no matter how much pressure he put on it. Maybe he could have survived the night with no water and a healthy shoulder. Maybe he could have dealt with the gunshot wound if he'd had some water. But a bleeding wound with no water? "That's two great tastes that taste great together," he said giggling, rapidly approaching delirium.

Tony would be dead by morning, and he knew it.

Which is why he was confused, at first, when a United States Air Force Blackhawk helicopter suddenly rose over the lip of the dune behind him.

Tony turned, stared . . . and fell over sideways.

He didn't quite lose consciousness—not quite— but things did get blurry. When the world came back into focus, Tony saw Rhodey hustling toward him down the slope of the dune.

"Saving you is getting to be a full-time job," Rhodey said when he reached Tony's side, a grin spreading across his face. "C'mon. Let's get you out of here."

"Pick my blood up off the sand as we go, would you?" Tony mumbled. "I think I need it."

Heat waves rose from the pavement at Edwards Air Force Base, shimmering and distorting the summer air, disguising the enormous mass of the approaching C-17 until its landing gear had touched down. The massive plane taxied in and came to a stop just outside a hangar.

The rear ramp shook and lowered, letting in the midday glare, causing both Tony Stark and James Rhodes to squint, turn their heads, and shade their eyes with their hands. Tony sat in a wheelchair, dressed in a set of ill-fitting scrubs, while Rhodey stood right behind him. Tony blinked, squinted, blinked again, and finally realized what he was seeing.

Revealed by the lowering ramp, Pepper Potts stood on the tarmac in front of Tony's waiting limousine, clutching her tablet computer to her chest like a security blanket. Her back was ramrod-straight, her hair and her clothes picture-perfect, her expression placid. But Tony had known her for far too long to miss the telltale signs: the barely perceptible tremor in her lower lip; the way she shifted her weight, ever so slightly, from one foot to the other; the color of her knuckles as they gripped the tablet.

Not that he'd ever let on that he noticed.

Rhodey wheeled him down the ramp, and as soon as they reached the bottom, Tony struggled to stand. "Help me out of this thing—"

His efforts proved to be more ambitious than he was ready for, as Tony faltered and almost fell. Rhodey was there in a flash, lifting his friend and steadying him.

"I've got you, pal."

Tony straightened, grateful for Rhodey's aid, and tried to appear as though he were standing under his own power as Pepper approached him. This wasn't easy, since he feared he might either tip over or faint at any moment.

The medic in the Blackhawk and the doctors aboard the transport plane all told him it was a miracle that he wasn't dead, given the amount of blood he'd lost and the blunt trauma that he'd somehow suffered over 90 percent of his body.

Tony decided not to tell them that he'd received those injuries while wearing a homemade suit of powered armor and destroying a few billion dollars' worth of his own products.

Pepper stopped a few paces in front of the men and made eye contact with Rhodey, her face still poised and all but unreadable. "Thank you," she murmured. Rhodey nodded to her solemnly.

Then she finally faced Tony, and all of the things he had noticed from the top of the ramp were still there, joined by an alarming gray pallor to her skin and the kind of puffiness around the eyes that could only have come from a long, sustained cry. Still, the smile she gave him was a brave one.

Tony returned it. "Your eyes are red. A few tears for your long-lost boss?"

Pepper's eyes twinkled, a testament to the strength that lay unshaken beneath the emotional turmoil. "Tears of joy. I hate job hunting."

Tony chuckled.

The driver's door of the limo opened and Hogan jumped out, hurrying to open the rear door. Tony made his way to the car carefully, still with Rhodey's help, and gave Hogan a friendly nod.

"Good to see you again, sir," Hogan said warmly.

Tony asked, "You do something new with your hair?"

"Wouldn't dream of it, sir."

Pepper took over and helped Tony into the limo. Rhodey grinned at him. "I'll catch up with you in a little while, okay?"

"You do what you've gotta do," Tony replied, sighing as he sank into the plush leather.

Rhodey nodded again at Pepper, then headed toward a waiting golf cart. Tony knew General Gabriel was expecting him.

Inside the limousine, Tony luxuriated in the air-conditioning, ran his hands over the upholstery, and sighed again. Hogan started the engine, but Tony gave no directions; he simply sat there, enjoying himself.

Pepper glanced up toward the front and met Hogan's eyes in the rearview mirror.

Hogan cleared his throat politely. "Where to, Mr. Stark?"

Pepper answered him. "We're due at the hospital."

"No." Tony opened his eyes and straightened up in

his seat. "To the office." Pepper started to protest, but Tony lifted a hand to stop her. "Relax, okay? The docs on the plane knew what they were doing. I'm as patched up as I'm going to get."

"Patched up or not, you need rest."

"Listen, Pepper. I've been in captivity for *months*. There are only two things I want to do. I want to eat a cheeseburger. And I want to hold a press conference."

"A *press conference*? You're joking."

"No joke."

"Why do you want to hold a press conference?"

"Don't people usually do that when they want to talk to the press?"

"But I don't—you mean *now*? You want to go from the airplane to a press conference."

Tony grinned. "I know these things take a little bit of time to set up, Pepper. Why don't we say . . . in two hours? That'll give you enough time to set everything up, won't it?"

While Pepper, beyond exasperated, struggled for words, Hogan put the car in gear and headed for the Stark Industries offices.

Chapter Twelve

When the limo pulled up to the main entrance of the central building at the Stark Industries headquarters, Tony Stark opened the door and climbed out. He still moved carefully, a bit laboriously, but his spirits were greatly improved. This was because of two things.

First, he was at that moment shoving the last bite of a juicy cheeseburger into his mouth. He didn't accept Hogan's arm getting out, but Tony did drop the fast-food wrappers into the driver's hands.

Second, instead of baggy scrubs, Tony now wore his favorite suit. They had dropped Pepper off first to make arrangements and then Tony had gone home to give himself a decent shave.

"I feel like a new man, Hogan," he said, as boisterously as he was able.

"I don't doubt it, sir," the driver answered, shutting the door behind his employer.

Waiting for Tony on the building's front steps was a large group of Stark employees, with Obadiah Stane standing in front of them and flashing a brilliant grin from ear to ear. Everyone started applauding as Obadiah opened his arms wide and went to Tony for a hug.

"See this?" Obadiah asked the crowd as he threw his arms around Tony. "Huh? Huh?"

Tony hugged him back. Dropping his voice so that only Tony could hear him now, Obadiah said, "Tony, I thought we were meeting at the hospital? You know, there are a lot of reporters in there. What's going on?"

Tony released him and stepped back with an enigmatic smile. "You'll see. C'mon."

The employees, still clapping and cheering, parted to let Tony and Obadiah through as they headed into the building.

In the headquarters lobby, which was indeed packed with reporters anxious to get a precious moment of Tony Stark's time, Pepper Potts stood off to one side watching the controlled frenzy. There were rows of chairs lined up in front of a podium where Tony intended to give this impromptu press conference, but no one sat. They all stood, ready to pounce the second Tony showed up.

Pepper saw one of them, a weathered-looking man in his forties, break free of the pack and start toward her but she tried not to acknowledge him. If any of the others saw her paying one reporter any significant attention, they'd all want some and she didn't have the time.

Before the man could speak to her, Pepper said,

"You'll have to take a seat, sir."

He favored her with a smile that stopped short of his eyes. "Oh, I'm not a reporter. I'm Agent Phil Coulson, with the Strategic Homeland Intervention, Enforcement, and Logistics Division."

She turned to look at him for the first time, her expression mildly skeptical. "Look, Mr. Coulson, we've already spoken with the DOD, the FBI, the CIA—"

He interrupted her. "We're a separate division with a more . . . specific focus. We need to debrief Mr. Stark about the circumstances of his escape. More importantly—"

Impatient, Pepper cut him off. "Well, great, I'll let him know."

But Coulson continued as if she hadn't said a word. "We're here to help. We're here to listen. I assure you, Mr. Stark will want to talk to us."

Pepper smiled back at him, unimpressed. "I'm sure he will. Now if you could just take your seat."

She turned her attention back to the huge front doors just as Tony and Obadiah Stane walked in together. The reporters mobbed, and Tony struggled his way through them to the podium.

Pepper immediately started worrying that Tony would push himself too far and collapse. She completely forgot about Agent Phil Coulson.

Finally reaching the podium, Tony leaned on it, staring silently at the crowd. Part of this was for effect, and it worked, as the reporters immediately stopped talking. Part of it was so he could catch his breath.

Tony stayed like that, simply staring at the assembled media, long enough for it to grow awkward. Obadiah, still completely in the dark about what was going on in Tony's head, had started up toward the podium to save him when at last Tony spoke.

"I . . . can't do this anymore."

And then further silence, but it was a charged silence as the import of Tony's words sank in. A few murmurs here and there, a few questions whispered through the crowd, and a reporter finally stood up and asked a direct question.

"You mean you're retiring?"

"No," Tony answered immediately. "I don't want to retire. I want to do something else."

Another reporter piped up. "Something besides weapons?"

"Yes, that's right."

Now the quiet murmurs and whispered questions exploded into a buzz like multiple chain saws. *Tony Stark not making weapons?* It was the sound of Big News.

The second reporter made herself heard again above the din. "The official report was sketchy. What happened to you over there, Mr. Stark?"

Tony hesitated, pensive. He glanced back at Obadiah, then met Pepper's eyes across the room. He took a deep breath.

"What happened over there? I had my eyes opened, that's what happened. I saw my weapons, with my name on them, in the hands of thugs. I thought we were doing good here . . . but I can't say that any-more."

Coming in from a rear entrance, Rhodey made his way over to Pepper, stopping beside her while he stared at Tony up at the podium. "Uh . . . weren't we taking him to the hospital?"

But Pepper didn't even hear him. She stood trans-fixed by what Tony was saying, and noticed nothing else. Especially not Agent Coulson, who stood nearby watching the whole scene.

The same reporter asked, "What do you intend to do about it, Mr. Stark?"

"The system is broken," Tony said, getting warmed up now. "There's no accountability whatsoever. Right now, as of this second, we are freezing the sale of all Stark weaponry worldwide."

The chaotic buzz that had overtaken the room ear-lier returned and became an uproar.

Caught completely off-guard by this announce-ment, Obadiah Stane shouldered his way toward Tony, his expression and body language indicating that he was more than ready to wrap the whole thing up.

Tony continued. "We've lost our way. I need to re-evaluate things. And my heart's telling me I have more to offer the planet than things that blow up."

Another reporter finally got a word in. "So you're saying—uh, what *are* you saying?"

Obadiah reached the podium, but rather than let the older man shoo him away and close the conference,

Tony put his arm around Obadiah and pulled him close in an awkward display of camaraderie. Obadiah tried his best not to look intensely uncomfortable.

"In the coming months, Mr. Stane here and I will set a new course for Stark Industries. 'Tomorrow, Today' has always been our slogan. It's time we try to live up to it."

The reporters started firing questions all at once then, generating a cacophonous wall of sound, and Obadiah finally succeeded in getting to the microphones.

"Okay, I think we're going to be selling a lot of newspapers here." The throng died down enough to hear him. "What we should take away from this is that Tony's back, he's healthier than ever, and as soon as he heals up and takes some time off, we're going to have a little internal discussion and get back to you. Thank you for coming by."

Tony had already left the podium, exhilarated. He made his way through the crowd to Pepper and Rhodey, both of whom stood with stunned looks on their faces.

Pepper asked, "Do you mean all that? Or is this some clever stock maneuver?"

Tony grinned. "Wait and see."

Later, after the reporters had all finally drifted away, Obadiah Stane found Tony Stark outside the Stark Industries ARK Reactor at the opposite end of the compound. Tony leaned against a decorative railing, his exquisite suit incongruous next to the paper soda cup in his hand and the order of fries he was eating.

Tony stared thoughtfully up at the hulking mass of the ARK Reactor. It was the most futuristic-looking of all the buildings in the compound, a glass, stone, and steel behemoth that seemed poised to usher in a new age of advanced technology.

Inside the building, behind two twelve-feet-thick walls of reinforced steel and concrete, lay the Reactor itself: a massive spire springing out of a vast pool of bubbling superheated plasma. It looked nothing like any other power plant on earth, and indeed *was* nothing like any other power plant.

The Reactor building seemed to be deserted. No foot traffic came in or out. No researchers were visible through its windows. Tony couldn't take his eyes off it. Silently he ate a fry and took a sip of his drink.

"That went well," Obadiah said, staring at the Reactor alongside Tony.

"Did I just paint a target on the back of my head?" Tony asked.

Obadiah glanced sharply at his employer. "*Your* head? What about *my* head? What do you think the over-under on the stock drop is going to be tomorrow?"

"Forty points."

Obadiah all but snorted. "*Minimum.* Tony, we are a weapons manufacturer."

"I don't want a body count to be our only legacy," Tony shot back, unperturbed.

"What we do here keeps the world from falling into chaos."

For the first time, Tony looked away from the Reactor and met Obadiah's eyes. "Well, judging from what I just saw, we're not doing a very good job. There are other things we can do."

"Like what?" Frustration crept into Obadiah's voice. "You want us to make baby bottles?"

"We could reopen development of Repulsor Technology."

Obadiah narrowed his eyes. "The ARK Reactor was a publicity stunt. We built it to shut the hippies up."

"It works," Tony said quietly.

"Yeah, as a science project. It was never cost effective. We knew that before we built it. Repulsor Technology is a dead end. Right?"

Tony set down the soft drink. "Maybe."

"But there haven't been any breakthroughs in thirty years." Stane paused, and a strange note crept in. "Right?"

Tony started to grin. "You're a lousy poker player. Who told you?"

Openly excited now, Obadiah said, "Come on, let me see the damn thing."

Teasing, Tony asked, "Was it Rhodey?"

Obadiah looked as if he might start jumping up and down. "Just show it to me!"

Tony popped his shirt open, revealing the glowing Repulsor unit nestled in his chest. He watched Obadiah Stane's face and could see the hundreds, maybe thousands of thoughts running through his mind.

When Obadiah spoke again, he had accepted the reality of the Repulsor device that kept Tony alive, and already had begun formulating courses of action. Tony appreciated Obadiah's ability to think on his feet like that. It made him glad he had a friend of Obadiah's caliber to count on.

"Well, everyone needs a hobby, I suppose," Obadiah said. By now he could have been discussing a fascination with model trains, for all the excitement in his voice. "Listen, we're a team. There's nothing we can't do if we stick together. No more of this ready-aim-fire business, all right? No more press. Can you promise me that?"

Tony adjusted his shirt, covering the Repulsor unit. "Maybe."

"Just, just let me handle this. Okay? I did it for your father, I'll do it for you. But please, you've got to lay low. Just for a while. Can you do that for me, at least?"

Tony picked up the soft drink cup and took a sip, thinking.

Chapter Thirteen

A few hours later, after darkness had fallen, Tony Stark walked into his home and watched it come alive.

Sensing Tony's presence, Jarvis turned on lights, shaded windows a certain way, fired up a truly enormous flat-screen television, and played soft, soothing music over the surround-sound system present in every room.

"Hello, Mr. Stark," Jarvis's voice said from everywhere.

"Hello, Jarvis."

"What can I do for you?"

Tony paused in his living room and looked around. His eyes settled on one of the big picture windows, but he wasn't really seeing it. "Jarvis . . . I need to build a better heart."

A pause, maybe a second and a half, as Jarvis searched for a response. "I'm not sure I follow, sir."

"Give me a scan and you'll see."

"Of course, sir. Shall I set up the 3D scanner in your workshop?"

"I'll meet you there."

"Very good, sir."

It only took twenty minutes to set the intricate machine up exactly the way Tony wanted it. Tony had used the imaging apparatus over the years to provide machining specs down to the tiniest possible margin of error, and had always been more than satisfied with its performance. He never expected to scan himself.

And yet there he stood, shirtless and wearing goggles, holding perfectly still as ruby-red lasers played over every inch of his body, mapping him exhaustively.

When the last of the data had been collected, Tony pulled off the goggles and glanced over at a bank of monitors nearby. Terabytes of data screamed past on every screen as Jarvis processed it.

"If I may ask, sir," Jarvis began tentatively, "what were your intentions for this device?"

Tony slipped a shirt on. "It powers an electromagnet which keeps the shrapnel in my chest from entering my heart. Can you recommend any upgrades?"

Another 1.5-second pause. "It is difficult to offer counsel, since your stated intentions are inconsistent with your actions."

The stream of data on one of the monitors shifted and resolved into a laser image of the Repulsor unit. The image separated into its various components on the screen as Jarvis analyzed each one.

"What're you talking about?" Tony demanded.

"That's ridiculous. That is *exactly* the purpose of this invention."

On the monitor, Jarvis delved deeper into the device, zooming in through different layers. As the image grew larger and larger, it began to resemble some sort of highly advanced alien city more than any kind of power source.

"Sir, the energy yield of this device outperforms your stated intention by eleven orders of magnitude. You could accomplish your stated goal with the power output of a car battery."

Data and calculations still flashed across all the other monitors at blinding speed.

"Upgrade recommendations," Tony said flatly. "List."

"Why are you talking to me like a computer?"

"Because *you* are acting like one."

Although he was only an artificial intelligence, Jarvis sounded slightly hurt. "Shall I disable random pattern conversation?"

"No. It's okay. You're the only one who understands me."

Without subtle irony audible in his voice, Jarvis said, "I don't understand you, sir."

Tony eyed the monitors, frowning. "Were you always this dry? I remember you having more personality than this."

"Shall I activate sarcasm harmonics?"

"Fine," Tony replied, impatient. "Could you please make your recommendations now?"

When Jarvis spoke again, the sarcasm practically

dripped off his words and puddled on the floor. "It would thrill me to no end."

Tony lost his frown. "Ahh. *That's* more like it."

Jarvis spent a few seconds compiling information. A laser printer near the monitors began filling its paper tray with sheets covered in technical specifications and schematics. "Recommendations complete. Shall I begin machining parts while you look over the data?"

Tony picked up the stack of papers and flipped through them. He grinned. "Machine away."

At one end of Tony's workshop stood a large device. Powered down, it could have been mistaken by someone with an untrained eye for any number of bulky metal items, from some sort of boiler to a high-tech portable barbecue. On the other hand, if it were seen by, say, an engineering student from MIT, the device would have caused a great deal of eye-bulging and mouth-watering. If that same engineering student were to see the device powered up and operating, he or she might well go into a fit of hysterics.

The device was the Stark Industries Series IX CNC Combo, a computer numerical control machine that incorporated a lathe, a milling center, and a set of robotic arms equipped with industrial plasma torches among dozens of other accessories. Only four Series IXs existed in the entire world. Only three clients had been wealthy enough to afford one. Tony loved the Series IX more than all of the thirty-seven sports cars in his personal parking deck combined.

The machine made a low, sweet hum as Jarvis powered it up. Jarvis's robotic arm, affixed to a mobility unit that allowed it to travel wirelessly anywhere in the workshop, came to life beside the Series IX and began organizing pieces of stock metal in a large bin. Selecting the perfect one, Jarvis fed it into one end of the machine and pulled back, watching, as the metal disappeared inside the housing. The Series IX CNC Combo could, if handled correctly, make anything.

Or at least that was how Tony thought of it. It was the ultimate in precision metal-crafting. Any gear, any cog, any engine part, any missile component.

Any piece of armor.

With the proper raw material and careful programming, the Series IX could fabricate a part so precisely that the margin of error more or less disappeared.

As hours passed and the CNC Combo machine worked, Tony made his own selections of the perfect pieces of metal, feeding them one by one into the Series IX. He never realized how broadly he was grinning as he worked.

Thousands of miles away, the air over the sand dunes was dead still. There was no wind, nor even any suggestion of wind. It was as if the atmosphere had become an immense dead weight, pressing down on the Afghan desert, crushing anything with the audacity to try to move beneath its overwhelming presence.

The metal fingers protruding from the sand seemed to lend credence to the air's determination—as though even a man made of iron had no hope of escape. The illusion was shattered, or at the very least diminished, when a dirty hand made of flesh and bone reached down and grabbed the metal fingers and pulled them up from the earth.

The hand belonged to a scrawny Afghan, who shook the metal gauntlet over his head, hooting in triumph. Beyond him, a mismatched group of horses and old, battered, near-death pickup trucks dotted the top of a large dune. Other men spread out from the vehicles, searching, combing through the bone-dry, dusty landscape.

One truck, a Toyota slightly less decrepit than the rest of them, was notable for three reasons. First, it was hung with a banner that displayed the symbol of the ten interlocking rings. Second, in the bed of the Toyota, the Afghans had mounted a large-caliber machine gun.

And third, in the truck bed, a large, muscular man in badly faded army fatigues leaned against the machine gun. Flies buzzed around his head, and he swatted them away with cold, deliberate motions.

The flies refused to leave. They were too tempted by the horrible, raw burn scars that covered Raza's head and neck. Raza tilted his head, refusing to acknowledge the pain this movement caused, and stared down at the object he held in his right hand, the object that seemed to stare back at him mockingly.

The mask of the Iron Man. The mask made by Tony Stark.

In Urdu, Raza bellowed, *"Keep looking. I want all of it."*

Chapter Fourteen

The morning after Tony Stark and Jarvis began their latest project in Tony's workshop, Pepper Potts knocked on Tony's bedroom door. When there was no answer, Pepper opened the door and cautiously went inside.

Tony's bed hadn't been touched. The huge TV was on, but Pepper didn't attribute much to that, since most of the televisions in the place were set to timers. She did pause for a moment when she realized what was playing: a financial show that gave out stock tips.

"Stark Industries!" the host all but shouted. "I've got one recommendation. Ready? SELL! Abandon ship! Does the *Hindenburg* ring any bells?" He jabbed a big red sound-effect button, and canned shrieking filled the bedroom.

Pepper turned the TV off when her cell phone rang. She answered on her way back out to the living room. "Potts here."

"Hello, this is Agent Coulson with Strategic Homeland Inter—"

Pepper cut him off. "Yes. I remember. What can I do for you?"

On the other end of the line, Agent Coulson sat behind his desk in a small, very plain, very standard government office. He had spread out several newspapers on the desktop, each one with a headline such as "STARK RAVING MAD?" or "STARK LUNACY." Coulson eyed the papers analytically, but his voice remained bland as he talked to Pepper.

"I've left a number of messages, Ms. Potts, trying to get something on the books with Mr. Stark." He reached out and picked up one of the papers, staring at the headline as if closer scrutiny would force it to divulge some hidden meaning.

"I know this is a priority for him," Pepper said, "but the next few weeks are a bit up in the air, and I can't set appointments without speaking with him first."

Coulson let the paper drop. "Do you know when you will be speaking with him again?"

Pepper hadn't left the living room. She told Coulson, "I'm not sure," and then almost yelped when Tony's voice echoed loudly out of the in-house intercom system.

"Pepper? How big are your hands?"

On the phone, Coulson asked, "What was that?"

"Agent Coulson, I really have to go. Let me get back to you later." She hung up, shot an exasperated look at the intercom, and said, *"What?"*

The speaker shot back, "How big are your hands?"

"I don't underst—"

But Tony had lost his patience with the conversation. "Just get down here, okay? I'm in the workshop."

Pepper didn't know what to expect when she reached the workshop, so she tried to prepare herself for anything.

It didn't work.

When she opened the door and walked in, Tony was the first thing she saw, and the breath caught in her throat. He sat in a chair across the room from her, shirtless . . . and the Repulsor device glowed in his chest. Pepper had heard Rhodey describe the Repulsor unit, but she hadn't seen it until now. She couldn't decide whether to scream and run, or just stand and stare.

Tony bypassed her reaction completely. "Show me your hands," he said, beckoning her forward.

Pepper hesitantly approached him and held out her hands.

"Perfect, they're small. I need you to help me."

Pepper couldn't take her eyes off the Repulsor unit. "So that's the thing that's keeping you alive."

"That's the thing that *was* keeping me alive. It is now an antique." Tony held up a newly fabricated, even higher-tech version of the device in his chest. "This is what *will* be keeping me alive for the foreseeable future."

"Amazing," Pepper said.

"I'm going to swap them out and switch all functions to the new unit."

122

Pepper found herself wanting to reach out and touch the new Repulsor unit, but she resisted the impulse. Instead she asked, "Is it safe?"

Tony nodded. "Completely." He gestured toward a box on a nearby counter. "Put on a pair of those sterile gloves, would you? First I need you to reach in and—"

Pepper took a startled step backward. "Reach into *where*?"

"The socket."

"What socket?"

He hooked a thumb toward his breastbone. "The chest socket. Listen carefully, because we have to do this in a matter of minutes."

"Or else what?"

"Or else I go into cardiac arrest."

Pepper's hand went to her mouth. "I thought you said it was safe."

"I didn't want you to panic."

Pepper identified the feeling suddenly spreading throughout her body as panic of the highest order. Tony could see her eyes widening in distress.

"Stay with me," Tony said sternly. "I need you to relieve the pressure on my myocardial nerve."

"I don't know how to do that!"

"I'm *telling* you how to do that."

Pepper latched onto the sound of Tony's even, calm, supremely confident voice and used it as an anchor. "Sorry . . ."

Tony shifted in the chair. "Listen. I'm going to lift off the old chest piece—"

Alarmed, Pepper blurted, "Won't that make you *die*?"

He sighed. "Not immediately. When I lift it off, I need you to reach into the socket as far as your hand can fit and gently move the housing away from my heart. Do you know what direction that is?"

"To the right."

"To *my* right. Your left."

She nodded. "To the left."

"Right."

"Left."

"Right," he said brusquely. "Left." Then he added, "Ready?"

Pepper took a few deep breaths. Then she put on a pair of the sterile gloves. "Ready."

She held her breath as Tony slowly, carefully removed the Repulsor unit from his chest, and did her best not to wince at the gaping, scar-edged hole it left behind. "Okay," he said. "Now."

Pepper started reaching in. Slowly, more and more of her hand disappeared inside Tony's chest. "How deep does this go?"

"Keep going."

Pepper kept reaching . . . and reaching . . . and her face squinched up more and more the deeper she went.

"That's it," he said encouragingly. "Deeper. *There.* Now press. Yes. It's releasing."

Pepper let out a sigh of relief and extracted her hand, which came out covered in a nasty pink slime. "Eww!" she exclaimed, horrified and alarmed. "Pus!"

"It's *not* pus." The impatience crept back into Tony's voice. "It's an inorganic plasmic discharge. It's from the device, not my body."

"Well, it smells. Am I done?"

"Yes. Thank you."

Pepper peeled off the gloves and dropped them into a wastebasket. She pointedly did not watch as Tony used a small tubelike apparatus to clean out the opening in his chest, but she couldn't help noticing Jarvis's robotic arm, which glided over and stopped next to Tony's chair.

"The new unit is much more efficient," Tony said as he worked. "This shouldn't happen again."

Pepper turned and leaned against a workbench. "Good, because it's not in my job description."

"Oh, yeah? It is now."

Pepper's eyes roamed around the workshop, finally settling back on her boss. She wondered briefly what she had done to end up with this life: standing in what amounted to a mad scientist's lair, reaching inside a man's chest so he could clamp on his new superpowered pacemaker. In an attempt to change the subject, she asked, "I don't suppose you want to go over things?"

Tony set the cleaning apparatus down and settled back into the chair. The robotic arm took that as its cue, picked up the new chest unit, and seated it snugly in Tony's chest socket.

"Can it at least wait until I install my new untested groundbreaking self-contained power source and lifesaving device prototype?"

Pepper winced, watching the robotic arm perform its functions. "I suppose." She drifted over and eyed the old Repulsor unit, now lying discarded on a nearby tabletop.

Tony saw what she was looking at. "Throw that thing out."

Surprised, she said, "Don't you want to save it?"

"Why? It's antiquated."

"You made it out of spare parts in a dungeon. It saved your life. Doesn't it have at least some nostalgic value?"

Tony ignored the robotic arm's activities as he spoke to Pepper; he could just as easily have been getting a shoe shine. "Pepper. I have been called many things. 'Nostalgic' is not one of them."

The arm withdrew, and the new Repulsor unit lit up brightly. "There," Tony said, satisfied. He stood up. "Good as new. Thank you."

"You're welcome," Pepper said with a note of reservation. "But can I ask you a favor?"

"Shoot."

She gestured at the Repulsor unit. "I don't do well under that kind of pressure. If you need someone to do something like that again, get somebody else."

Tony took a step forward, reaching for a shirt lying over the back of a nearby chair. The movement put him just inside what Pepper considered her personal space, and she was about to move backward, but then Tony said something that stopped her.

"Pepper—I don't have anyone else."

The words were simple, but they struck Pepper as profoundly honest, true, and sad. Suddenly she was very aware of Tony's skin and the outlines of his muscles and the depth of his dark, intelligent eyes.

But then she took a step backward, cleared her throat, and asked, "Will that be all, Mr. Stark?"

He dropped his eyes to the shirt in his hands. "That will be all, Miss Potts."

Pepper turned and left the workshop. She didn't look back, and so she didn't see how closely Tony watched her go.

Tony rarely left his workshop in the days that followed. He kept up his personal hygiene reasonably well—not a big surprise, given the overt luxury of the custom-built, mountain-stone-lined, seven-jet walk-in shower in his bathroom—but he slept in his bed one night out of five, if that. He communicated with Pepper and the rest of the outside world either by intercom or by phone. He had all his food delivered.

A week had passed since Pepper had helped him replace the Repulsor unit in his chest. Tony spread a stack of schematics out over one of his spacious worktables. Then he picked up a soldering gun and continued work on his latest item: a pair of sculpted metal boots.

Silently, Jarvis's robotic arm glided up behind him and "looked" over his shoulder. A tiny camera mounted on the arm's manipulator whispered almost silently as it adjusted its focus to peer at the boots.

Jarvis's voice emerged from the room's hidden speakers. "Still having trouble walking, sir?"

"These aren't for walking," Tony mumbled, intent on his work.

The arm withdrew, and for the next few hours, no one spoke. When he finally felt satisfied with his progress, Tony grabbed a roll of electrical tape, cleared out a space on the workshop's floor, and began laying down strips in a wide circle.

Then he buckled a nylon-and-metal "bandolier" around his torso with a small but heavy control module attached to it. Wires ran from the control module to the two metal boots, which Tony now slipped onto his feet. He stood and walked into the center of the circle, his footsteps loud and heavy, like the sound made by a machine. In his hands were two wireless controllers that looked a lot like joysticks.

"Ready to record the big moment, Jarvis?"

"All sensors ready, sir."

Tony stood up as straight as he could, lifted the two joysticks, and activated thumb buttons on both. A familiar blue glow—the same glow that emanated from the second-generation Repulsor unit in his chest—erupted from beneath the boots and propelled Tony straight up into the air.

The glow continued as Tony immediately lost control, flipped over sideways, and jetted straight into a pile of scrap metal heaped against one wall.

The monitors filled up with so much data, moving so quickly, that they blurred and became shifting walls of color. Dryly, Jarvis announced, "That flight yielded excellent data, sir."

Tony groaned and shifted on the scrap pile. "Great." He got to his feet, acutely aware of a dozen places that would be black-and-blue by the time he ate his next meal. "I, uh, I think I know what this needs."

Chapter Fifteen

The next afternoon was another California day of sunshine and cloudless skies. Rhodey stood in a hangar at Edwards Air Force Base, lecturing to a group of student pilots. He paced back and forth in front of an F-22 fighter jet, which sat beside a remote-piloted Global Hawk drone.

Rhodey didn't let it show, but he lived for these moments. He was still a young man, but James Rhodes had seen more things, been more places, and accomplished much, much more than most soldiers twice his age. Throughout Desert Shield and the Iraq War, Rhodey had consistently gone above and beyond in operation after operation, both public and covert. He had a safe filled with medals to show for it.

These days, since he had taken the job as liaison to Stark Industries, his field operations had been all but eliminated. Rhodey figured that was fair.

"If I can pass any of my experience along to the kids coming up," he once told Pepper, "even just a shred of it. If I can get them to learn from my mistakes and the mistakes of the people I've served with, instead of having to make their own, well, then I can die happy."

Pacing back and forth in the hangar, Rhodey dragged his gaze from one face to another, playing the stern instructor. It worked. He had the undivided attention of every student there.

"Manned or unmanned," he began. "Which is the future of air combat?" Without giving them a chance to pipe up, he continued. "For my money, no drone, no computer will ever trump a pilot's instincts. His reflexes, his judgment—"

A familiar voice chimed in from deep inside the hangar. "Why not take it a step further?"

Rhodey looked around, pleasantly surprised. He made sure *that* didn't show on his face, either, as Tony Stark strolled out of the shadows and approached the class.

"Why not"—Tony paused for effect—"a pilot *without* the plane?"

"That I'd like to see," Rhodey said. He couldn't help grinning. "Look who fell out of the sky."

Eyes twinkling, Tony addressed the students while he gestured toward the fighter jet and the drone beside it. "Who wants to take these apart and put them back together?"

Rhodey put the kibosh on that thought before anyone could respond. "All right, let's wrap it up."

The students trickled out, some of them disappointed, others simply confused, and all of them stealing looks at Tony. Rhodey turned to face his friend. "I didn't think I'd be seeing you for a while."

"Why not?"

"Figured you'd need a little time."

"Why does everybody think I need time?"

Rhodey shifted his weight and glanced around. "You've been through a lot. Thought maybe you should get your head straight."

"I've *got* it straight. And I'm back to work."

Rhodey's eyebrows lifted half an inch. "Really?"

"I'm onto something big," Tony said, quietly excited. "I want you to be a part of it."

"A lot of people around here will be happy to hear that." Rhodey sounded relieved. "What you said at that press conference really threw everyone."

Tony's face darkened. He put added emphasis on each word: "I mean what I said."

Rhodey shook his head. "No, you don't. You took a bad hit. It spun you around."

Tony's eyes narrowed. Rhodey's blatant dismissal hung there, tense, between them. When Tony spoke again, his voice came out brittle. "Maybe I do need a little time."

"All right then. Good seeing you."

"Likewise."

Tony turned and walked out of the hangar, away from Rhodey, his expression unreadable.

Tony retreated into his workshop again after his attempt to reach out to Rhodey, resuming his habits of sleeping there and only emerging to bathe. The CNC Combo machine ran almost constantly, and the monitors placed around the workshop flickered nonstop with streams of compressed data.

Early on a Wednesday afternoon, thanks to the arrival of a certain package, Pepper decided to brave the workshop again and made her way down from the main house, the package tucked under her arm. She knocked on the door, and when no one answered she went ahead and opened it, wondering what craziness or bizarre spectacle she might see this time.

Tony stood at the main workbench, a sculpted metal gauntlet on his right hand. Wires ran from the gauntlet to the same bandolier-mounted control module he had used before, which Pepper had seen lying around the workshop.

Tony raised the gauntlet, aimed the palm of the metal glove at the other end of the workbench, and released a burst of blue light, the same blue light that the chest unit emanated. A heavy toolbox flipped off the end of the bench and crashed to the floor, scattering tools everywhere.

Pepper had never seen anything like it. She came a little closer. "I thought you were done with weapons?"

Tony didn't look at her as he responded. "It's not a weapon. It's a flight stabilizer."

The contraption made her nervous, even when Tony disconnected the gauntlet, pulled it off, and set it on the bench. "Well, watch where you're pointing your 'flight stabilizer,' would you?" He didn't answer. "Obadiah's upstairs. Should I tell him you're in?"

Finally he looked her in the eye. "Be right up."

Pepper nodded and set the package—an oblong parcel about the size of a shoe box—on a nearby chair and made her way out without saying a word about it.

Tony eyeballed the box. He wasn't expecting anything. It wasn't his birthday. He went over and picked it up, hefted it, shook it, and listened to it. When it continued to divulge nothing in the way of clues, he finally tore it open.

"Well," he said softly, holding up the box's contents. Mounted inside a Lucite block was his original Repulsor chest unit, still glowing faintly. And below that, inscribed into the block itself, were the words, "PROOF THAT TONY STARK HAS A HEART."

Tony grinned in spite of himself.

A few minutes later, Obadiah Stane set an extra-large pizza down on the marble coffee table in Tony Stark's living room while Tony paced back and forth, full of manic energy. A bottle of red wine and two glasses stood beside the pizza box, as yet untouched.

Now, watching Tony stump back and forth across his $28,000 imported rug, Obadiah wondered what had really happened to Tony in Afghanistan.

"This is *the* big idea," Tony said, his voice bubbling with enthusiasm. "It can pull the company in a whole new direction."

"That's great," Obadiah said around a mouthful of

pizza. "Get me the design as soon as you can. We've got a hungry production line that could knock out a prototype in days."

Tony stopped and faced Obadiah. In that moment, whatever barrier of self-defense he had built between himself and the world around him might as well not have existed at all. "You know, I had a moment there where I was . . . reluctant . . . but I know now I made the best decision. I feel like I'm doing something . . . *right*, finally." His voice got a little thick. "Thank you for supporting me in this."

Obadiah nodded, surprised and touched by Tony's sincerity. "Listen, Tony, I have something to talk to you about. I really wish you'd attended the last board meeting like I asked you to."

Tony thought about sitting down, but remained standing. He still had too much energy. "I know, I'm sorry. What did I miss?"

Regretfully, Obadiah said, "The board's filed an injunction against you."

That stopped Tony cold. "What?"

"They claim you're unfit to run the company and want to lock you out."

After only a brief pause, Tony's manic energy returned, now transformed into outrage. "How can they do that? It's my name on the building! My ideas that drive that company!"

"They're going to try. We'll fight them, of course."

Tony frowned. "With the amount of stocks we own, I thought we controlled the company."

Obadiah shrugged. "I don't know. Somehow they pulled enough votes together. Listen, the world doesn't share your vision, Tony. The more people have to lose, the more frightened they are of new ideas."

He opened the bottle of wine, poured some in each glass, and offered one to Tony. Tony declined with a distracted gesture.

"Now listen," Obadiah went on, "I don't want you to get all in knots. You know how many times I protected your father from the wolves?"

Tony nodded silently, staring at a spot on the wall with unfocused eyes.

"Get back to your lab and work some magic. You let me handle the board. Oh, and Tony? No more press conferences."

Tony reluctantly nodded again.

Chapter Sixteen

Days began to pass with startling speed for Tony Stark. He spent so much time in his workshop and was so distracted when he was outside the workshop, that he completely lost track of the date and often the hour. He only spoke to Pepper on the phone; he hadn't spoken to Rhodey at all in . . . how long? He didn't know.

But none of that mattered, because things were starting to come together.

If Tony had to guess, he would have said it was a Sunday morning when he first assembled the belt, the boots, and the gauntlets. Tony stood in the middle of the workshop, the sculpted metal propulsion boots on his feet, the armored gauntlets on his hands, and a stabilizer belt buckled around his waist. All of the pieces were connected by an explosion of wires and tubing, bunching and coiling around Tony's body so that he looked like a walking science experiment.

"Ready, Jarvis?" he called out.

"Still rejecting my suggestion of a crash helmet, I see," the computer said, dry as dust.

"Still not needing one," Tony replied. "Begin recording."

"Recording, sir. Whenever you're ready."

Tony activated a switch on the stabilizer belt. Slowly, the propulsion boots glowed brighter and brighter blue and Tony lifted off the ground. He hovered in the air, tentative, feeling his way, and when he began to tilt forward he fired the gloves to compensate.

They worked perfectly.

Not that his balance was perfect; Tony tilted and weaved, firing judicious bursts of Repulsor energy from the gloves, trying hard not to overcompensate. For a minute, maybe two, he seemed to surf in midair, working to find his balance.

Gradually it came to him. Once he had steadied himself, Tony carefully tilted forward, just enough to provide some lateral motion. Before he realized it, Tony was gliding along the floor of the lab, as if slipping down a perfectly frictionless slide.

Tony torqued his body, fired a burst from the right glove, and dodged around the chair Pepper had set his surprise package on. The chair flipped over as he passed, knocked sideways by the Repulsor burst, but he considered that part of the learning curve.

Stabilizing with the right glove sent him skidding to the left, but he corrected his course, shifted his balance, and fired a burst from the left gauntlet. All of the tools and schematics went flying off a workbench, but Tony stayed upright and in control.

138

Describing a perfect arc, Tony skirted around the CNC Combo machine—missing it by less than an inch—and headed back toward the center of the workshop.

"Nothing to it," he whispered, his eyes twinkling.

Tony cut the propulsion and landed, relatively softly, on the workshop floor. He looked around until he saw Jarvis's camera-equipped robotic arm, which had taken cover behind the stock metal bin. The arm saw Tony looking at it and straightened up.

"All right," Tony said. "Let's get to work."

"Very good, sir. And if I may so, sir, I had every faith in your abilities."

Nevertheless, the robotic arm waited until Tony had disconnected the boots before it emerged from its cover.

On the other side of the planet, a large mud-colored tent flickered like a Japanese lantern in the darkness, lights burning brightly in its interior.

Inside the tent, a metallic monster had begun to take shape: a gray, fragmented nightmare painstakingly reassembled and now standing upright on a crude metal frame. Tony Stark's original armor, which he had spent so long building in the confines of the Afghan cave, now stared across the tent with hollow, menacing eyes and a gaping hole where its heart should be.

Filthy, sleep-deprived insurgents scurried about it, constantly working.

Across the tent, perched on a makeshift chair, Raza sat and watched the armor, fascinated as more and more pieces found their way back into the metallic jigsaw puzzle. He felt a certain kinship with the battered armor.

The horrible wounds inflicted on him by the flame-throwers built into this very suit had healed now, or at least scarred over. They no longer wept and oozed and drew flies. But his features hadn't returned to what a human face was supposed to look like. Raza was now a creature of nightmare himself, his skin a Halloween monster mask fitted tightly over his skull.

One of the insurgents brought in a metal gauntlet. Two other men immediately set about attaching it to the suit's wrist.

Raza sat and stared, mesmerized.

Seven more days passed. An outside observer would have been hard-pressed to prove that Tony Stark's palatial home was occupied at all, the house stood so quietly. No one came or went; no cars approached or left; no lights burned aboveground.

But down below, in his workshop, Tony toiled like a man possessed.

Even Pepper and Rhodey had been forbidden to trespass on Tony's marathon session with his machines and tools. The entire world seemed to shrink into a needle-sharp focus: Tony, Jarvis, and the metallic creation to which Tony was poised to give birth. The universe consisted of those three things, suspended in a limbo of carbon-alloy steel, embedded electronics, and the brilliant blue glow of the Repulsor unit above Tony's heart.

Now and then the reality of his situation reasserted itself, usually when he caught sight of his reflection in a mirror. Tony knew that the dozens of barbed, hooked, razor-sharp pieces of shrapnel in his chest were there to stay. The danger of removing them surgically was even greater than the risk of leaving them in place. The only way he could hope to survive was simply to prevent them from doing any more damage than they already had.

He also knew that if his electromagnetic lifeline were ever removed, it wouldn't take long for the shrapnel barbs to begin puncturing his cardiac tissue . . . first impairing the heart's function, then piercing it completely. If that happened, Tony would be dead in seconds from massive, irreversible internal bleeding.

The barbs would shred his heart.

But that looming specter didn't stop Tony from finishing what he had come to think of simply as "the prototype."

And on the evening of the seventh day, footsteps the likes of which the earth had never heard before echoed out of his underground workshop.

Something moved through the patches of light and shadow leading out through the work area, past the parked cars. Someone watching would only have seen a few tantalizing, terrifying glimpses as rays of fluorescent illumination glinted off isolated parts of the whole: thick, powerful arms and legs . . . steel vertebrae . . . scaly, metallic skin . . . all of it given an eerie shimmer by the flickering blue glow emanating from the breastplate.

The metal figure stopped and turned its head, then lifted its arms in a stretching motion, as if flexing the metal scale-covered muscles of its iron physique. Triggered by and in sync with these movements, air brakes and ailerons popped up from concealed panels along the figure's limbs and back.

It took another step forward and revealed its almost featureless face: the mouth was a grim horizontal slash, the glowing eyes deep-set in a harsh, flat metal plate.

Yet another step brought the figure into full illumination as it stopped beneath a ceiling-mounted spotlight. Tony flexed again, reveling in the sensation.

"This is it, Jarvis," he said, his voice distorted from inside the helmet. "The Mark II. Fully functional."

"But hardly finished, is it, sir?" Jarvis intoned.

Tony paused to look at his reflection in a car window. Jarvis had a point. The suit he wore now improved on the one he had built in the cave in the same way that a 747 airliner improved on the Wright Brothers' first flying machine, but it still lacked a lot of finishing touches. The seams and rivets still showed plainly. The suit's final exoskeleton had yet to be applied.

Not that that was going to stop Tony from performing as many tests as possible.

The suit began to hum as Tony powered up the

Repulsor generator. "Stand-by for calibration."

"Ready when you are, sir."

The blue radiance appeared at the propulsion outlets of the boots and at the palms of the gauntlets. When Tony increased the power output, the propulsion jets flared and he rose several inches off the floor of the garage.

"Nice," Tony murmured to himself. He started to turn . . . and something went wrong with his weight distribution. He tried to correct it, but with a spectacularly loud impact Tony fell over backward and landed squarely on the hood of a sports car, crushing it.

The car's alarm went off. Tony lifted one hand and fired a Repulsor burst, punching a sizable hole through the wrecked car's hood and silencing the alarm.

"We should take this outside," he said, ungracefully climbing out of what had suddenly become a $400,000 paperweight.

"Outside, sir?" Jarvis said, alarmed. "I must strongly caution against that. There are terabytes of calculations still needed—"

Tony cut him off. "We'll do them in-flight." He headed for the garage door, his metal boots echoing like distant thunder.

"Sir, the suit has not even passed a basic wind-tunnel test!"

Tony opened the door and stepped out into the night air. "That's why you're coming with me." Inside the helmet, a heads-up display (HUD) came to life, presenting Tony with a floating, easily accessed array of information. In the bottom center, a progress bar suddenly appeared and began filling from left to right, the words "JARVIS loading" hovering above it.

When the progress bar finished, Jarvis's voice spoke quietly but distinctly into Tony's ears. "Well, sir, now that I am indeed accompanying you on this mad venture, I suggest you allow me to employ Directive Four."

Tony powered up the suit again, lifted off, and hovered two feet off the ground. Slowly and carefully, he maneuvered along the length of the workshop's driveway, which led away from the back of the mansion.

"Directive Four. Isn't that, 'Never interrupt me when I'm with a beautiful woman?'"

"That's Directive Six. Directive Four: Use any and all means to protect your life should you be incapable of doing so."

"Whatever floats you, Jarvis."

Tony lifted his head and stared up into the star-filled sky. Then he took a deep breath, steadied himself with the gauntlets, and spiked the Repulsor output to near-maximum.

The suit shot into the sky like a missile wrapped in blue flame as Tony howled in pure, childlike delight. That delight faded a bit as Tony immediately lost his balance, tumbled about in the darkness over the coast, and struggled to right himself and regain control. The HUD remained steady, dutifully displaying altitude, power level, and vital signs among other data—but the numbers it showed him spun up and down so fast they became a distracting blur.

It didn't help that the horizon, visible through the HUD, whirled and trembled crazily.

"Sir, perhaps reaching a lower altitude is in order?" Jarvis said, without even a hint of sarcasm.

"Almost . . ." Tony said between gritted teeth. "Almost . . . got it . . ."

Tony hit an air pocket and spun like a top. It felt as if his brain were about to come out the back of his head, but he fought down a brief surge of panic and concentrated: skydivers stabilize themselves, they stabilize and dive. He had even done it himself a few times. Tony had to get lower, out of this turbulence. He tucked his arms back, tightened his legs, thrust out his chest . . . and found the answer.

Somewhere in his memory, some bit of information floated to the surface, chipping loose from a long-forgotten lecture involving gyroscopic balance and rocket propulsion: the Delta Pose. The perfect balance of thrust and control, legs straight and arms back in a V formation. Tony found his own Delta Pose, and it was as if the suit itself had come alive, realized what it had done wrong, and now strove to correct its errors.

Tony banked and turned, exploring, rocketing along the craggy coastline. He dipped lower, relishing the smooth control, reveling in the sensations. This went beyond anything any car or plane had ever given him. Tony soared over the ribbon of the Pacific Coast Highway, a radiant blue ghost fifty feet above the endless string of headlights.

He veered away from the road, from the land, carved a turn out over the ocean, and dived. The waves flashed by beneath him, splitting and shattering in his wake, and he turned again, heading back to shore. It was too much to contain. Tony whooped again, his pleasure pure and true, like a child on his first roller-coaster.

No one had ever felt this before. No one had ever experienced this before. Tony lost himself in the speed, the roar of the wind, the delicious chill of the night air.

He whipped upward into a high-performance climb, noting only vaguely that he was zooming past the Santa Monica Pier. He got close enough to the ferris wheel for a little boy in one of the cars to spot him, and though they were much too far away to make true eye contact, Tony felt a sudden and powerful kinship with the boy, as if he could see in the child a reflection of himself.

Tony climbed higher, leaving the pier behind, rising and at the same time sinking deeper and deeper into the joyous reverie his flight had brought him.

Clouds drew closer as he continued to climb. He disappeared into them, lost to sight, until a blue glow grew brighter and brighter at the clouds' upper surface and he burst free, a steel Icarus reaching for the heavens.

Ice crystals began to form on Tony's mask.

"Power levels have dropped to fifteen percent, sir. Recommend you descend and recharge."

On some level Tony knew Jarvis was talking to him, but he didn't hear the words. He climbed higher and higher still.

Increasing decibel levels, Jarvis said, "Sir? Sir! Acknowledge, Mr. Stark!"

Tony was somewhere else. The only thing he could see was the moon, high in the sky, huge and impossibly bright. A part of him wanted to reach it. *Intended* to.

Abruptly all of the readouts in the HUD began flashing red. Jarvis all but shouted, "Power at five percent! Threshold breached—"

Jarvis cut off as a loud *pop* filled Tony's helmet. Everything went dark except for the words "SYSTEM SHUTDOWN" flashing in front of his eyes.

Finally Tony snapped out of it. "Uh, Jarvis? *Jarvis . . . ?*"

But the glow had vanished from Tony's chest. He couldn't move his limbs. The suit had become a dead hull and its momentum finally ran out. Tony flipped upside down and dropped, headfirst, toward the ground tens of thousands of feet below.

Tony swallowed hard and tried to think. Not an easy task, with his stomach roiling in the nauseating free fall, but he kept his presence of mind sufficiently to shout, "Status, status! Reboot! *Reboot—*"

Another loud *pop*, and the blue Repulsor chest plate flared like a small blue sun. The HUD lit up again, and Tony's arms and legs responded when he tried to move them.

Before he could attempt any action, Jarvis's voice filled his head, infused with a sternness Tony had never heard before. "Temporary power restored, *sir*. Descend *immediately*."

Tony fired bursts from the gauntlets, flipping him upright again, then powered up the propulsion boots enough to regain some semblance of control. A map of the area flickered into the HUD, the location of Tony's mansion flashing in red. He navigated toward it.

"Jarvis, I think we need to chat about, uh, Directive Four."

"May I remind you, sir, that the suit feeds off the same power source as your life-support. A zero-drain of Repulsor energy will likely kill you."

Tony sighed. "You're a downer, Jarvis. But I appreciate the heads-up."

"You are *most* welcome, sir."

It only took a few minutes to get back to the Stark estate. Tony descended, aiming to make an elegant touchdown on the workshop driveway, but a few hundred feet off the ground it occurred to him that he had never actually come in for a landing before. He struggled, trying to find the proper landing pose.

"Shall I take over, sir?" Jarvis asked politely.

"No, I've got it, I've got it," Tony said, right before he crashed through the roof of the mansion. His descent completely unchecked now, he plunged through the foyer ceiling, smashed through the floor, emerged from the ceiling of his workshop, and utterly flattened another sports car.

Every car alarm in the garage went off.

Groaning, Tony sat up, pulled off the helmet, surveyed the destruction around him, and grinned.

"Perfect," he said. "Let's do some upgrades."

Chapter Seventeen

Soon Tony stood in his workshop, wearing scrub pants and a tank top, jazzed and typing rapidly on an array of keyboards he'd gathered around himself. His eyes flicked from monitor to monitor, taking in massive amounts of data, his mind whirring just as fast as Jarvis's processors. A plasma screen TV played nearby, set to mute, but Tony ignored it. Every now and then, without realizing it, he hummed a tuneless song.

The suit of armor hung on a rack nearby. Without Tony, and without the light of Tony's Repulsor "heart," it seemed not just empty but even sad, like the cast-off skin of a molting snake.

Despite Tony's upbeat mood, Jarvis took a disapproving tone. Considering that his voice emanated from every one of the sixteen speakers mounted unobtrusively around the workshop, this had an impressive effect. "That was quite dangerous, sir. Might I remind you—again—that if the suit loses power, so does your heart."

Tony didn't stop typing. "Yeah, and it doesn't have a seat belt, either. A few issues: Main transducer felt sluggish at plus forty altitude. Same goes for hull pressurization. I'm thinking icing might be a factor."

Jarvis let himself be distracted from his scolding by the technical conversation. "The suit isn't rated for high altitude. You're expending eight percent power just heating and pressurizing."

Tony switched to a different keyboard, this one hooked to a brand-new super-tower on a separate system from Jarvis. "Reconfigure using the gold-titanium alloy from the Seraphim Tactical Satellite. It should ensure fuselage integrity to fifty thousand feet, while maintaining power-to-weight ratio."

Tony's fingers flew across the keys. The computer's fans kicked up to a higher level as he challenged its processors.

"Shall I render, utilizing proposed specifications?"

Tony took another ten seconds to finish his computations and then hit the ENTER key, sending all of them to Jarvis. "Wow me."

The center screen in the array of monitors lit up, its endless stream of data vanishing to be replaced by a new figure, rapidly filling in from a wire-frame to a photorealistic image.

Tony let out a low whistle. "We've come a long way from that gray bucket-headed number I put together in Afghanistan, haven't we?"

"With all due modesty, sir, you didn't have *me* in Afghanistan."

150

"So that's the Mark III suit."

"Do you approve, sir?"

Tony ran his eyes over the Mark III, from the graceful curve of the shins to the heavy-industry hip joints, from the banded, pseudo-medieval plating across the arms and abdomen to the stern, sleek, otherworldly faceplate. The entire suit glittered a brilliant gold.

"Bit ostentatious, don't you think?"

He glanced around. It only took a second for his gaze to settle on his motorcycle with a custom paint job.

Inspired, Tony said, "Add a little red, would you?"

He would have continued chatting with Jarvis, but the TV caught his eye. The news had come on at some point, and a local entertainment reporter stood in front of the downtown concert hall. Tony hunted for the remote, grabbed it, and turned up the volume.

"Thank you, Jan," the reporter said. "Tonight's Red-Hot Red Carpet is here at the concert hall, where Tony Stark's third annual benefit for the Firefighter Family Fund has become the go-to charity gala on L.A.'s high-society calendar. But this great cause is only part of the story—"

The lab suddenly sprang to life as Jarvis started up various machines, including the CNC Combo, and the collective noise drowned out the reporter's voice. Tony sighed in annoyance and cranked the volume higher.

"—the man whose name graces the gold-lettered invitations hasn't been seen in public since his highly controversial press conference, and rumors abound.

Some say Stark is suffering from post-traumatic stress and hasn't left his bed in weeks."

Tony curled his lip, losing interest, and hit the MUTE button again before returning his attention to the central monitor: Jarvis had obligingly added a deep shade of red to the Mark III armor's design. The result was undeniably striking.

"The work could take till morning to complete, sir," Jarvis said tentatively.

"Good." Tony threw a sour glance at the TV. "I should come up for air anyway."

As Tony turned and left the lab, Jarvis's robotic arm sprang to life and began feeding slabs of metal into the Combo.

The sign read FIREFIGHTER FAMILY FUND. It was printed in black letters on a white background that sparkled silver every time the light from a flashbulb hit it, which was about once every two seconds.

A fire truck parked nearby set the tone for the evening as the red carpet ran past it—and on that red carpet, Obadiah Stane smiled, waved, and posed for the paparazzi, nodding and making eye contact with better than half the crowd watching.

It was an important crowd. The kind of crowd attracted by Stark Industries: politicians. Generals. "Kingmakers," they were sometimes called, the kind of people who never sought the spotlight, and in so doing became more powerful than any elected leader. Film stars and multiplatinum-selling recording artists mingled in the throng, unaware of their own relative triviality.

Obadiah moved along, heading for the entrance, away from the dark car just pulling up.

Tony Stark emerged, wearing an Italian suit even more expensive than the one he'd lost overseas. Every head swiveled and every camera came to focus on him. Tony flashed his "genuine" smile for them.

Tony caught up with Obadiah, who was much farther along the red carpet now, and moved up next to his old friend. He slid an arm around him, causing Obadiah to jump.

"What are you doing here?" Obadiah demanded. "I thought you were going to lay low."

Tony grinned, dropped the arm, and waved at a pretty reporter. "It's time to start showing my face again."

Skeptical, Obadiah said, "Let's just take it slow, okay? I've got the board right where we want them."

"Yeah, okay. I'll see you inside, all right? We've got lots to talk about."

Tony left Obadiah there and entered the hall.

Inside, in the grand ballroom where the function was being held, Tony crossed the floor to the bar. A tuxedo-clad band on a raised dais played jazz, and many of the richly clad attendees danced. It seemed to Tony, as he made his way through the crowd, that everyone not dancing was staring at him. He tried to tune them out as he ordered a drink.

An unfamiliar voice called out from behind him. "Mr. Stark."

Tony turned to look at the bland, stone-faced man who had addressed him. "Yes?"

Without extending his hand, the man said, "Agent Coulson."

Tony took his drink and thanked the bartender. "Was I supposed to meet you here, Agent Coulson?"

"No, but you haven't been returning my calls. This is serious. We need to get something on the books or I'll have to go official on you."

Tony's line of sight wavered from Coulson's face up and over the man's shoulder, then to a flight of stairs at one end of the ballroom that he spotted Pepper walking down. She was dressed in a long, shimmering, classically cut gown, her hair loose and flowing around her shoulders.

For a moment, Tony forgot that Agent Phil Coulson existed at all, and when Coulson cleared his throat and reaffirmed his own existence, Tony discovered he didn't care.

"Yes, Agent Coulson, you're right. I'm going to handle this right now. Let me check with my assistant." He shoved his drink into Coulson's hand and brushed past him, making a beeline for Pepper.

Pepper's eyes widened when she spotted Tony, just as surprised to see him as Obadiah had been, though less unpleasantly so.

"Miss Potts," Tony said, before she had a chance to speak, "can I have five minutes? You look . . . you look like you should always wear that dress."

"Thanks," she responded demurely. "It was a birthday present. From you."

"I have great taste," he replied appreciatively. "Care to dance?" Before she had a chance to say no, Tony took Pepper's hand and whisked her out onto the dance floor.

Pepper started to say, "Since when do you know how to dance?" but it only took a few steps to realize that Tony was, in fact, a *splendid* dancer.

Pepper let him take the lead. It wasn't difficult. She quickly saw that, like so many other things, dancing was something Tony had mastered long ago, then acted as if he cared nothing for it. Following him felt . . . natural. Felt *good*. Other couples began to watch them.

Tony spun Pepper gracefully around, then pulled her close. Color rose in her cheeks.

"I'm sorry," he said quietly. "Am I making you uncomfortable? You seem very uncomfortable."

Her eyes narrowed, but her mouth wanted to grin. "No, I *always* forget to wear deodorant and dance in a chiffon dress with my boss in front of everyone I've ever worked with."

They turned and spun with exquisite grace. "Would it help if I fired you?"

"You wouldn't last a week without me."

His eyebrows twitched up. "I'm not so sure."

"What's your Social Security number?"

Tony smiled, caught. "Uh . . ."

"That proves my point," she said, and found herself unable to repress a smile.

Together the two of them drifted outside onto the hall's veranda. They leaned against the railing, side by side, gazing up at the stars.

"I'm sorry I was so uncomfortable," Pepper murmured. Tony turned and was about to respond, but her words began to come out in a self-conscious rush. "I hate being the center of attention like that and that's why this one time in high school when I was supposed to be in a play . . . no, never mind . . . but you know that's why I never, like, wanted to have a big wedding . . . you know, because I thought everyone would be looking at me wearing a dress." She realized she'd used the word *wedding*. "Oh, no, no . . . I'm not saying, like, 'wedding.' No, not like that. I'm just saying, you know——"

Tony interrupted the torrent by leaning in and planting a kiss on Pepper's mouth. The kiss lingered, then broke . . . and it was as though all the sound in the world vanished when their lips parted.

They stood there, close but not touching, until just before the silence would have become awkward. Tony saved the moment: "Can I get you another glass of wine?"

Pepper turned around and leaned the small of her back against the railing. "What you can get me is a vodka martini, extra dry, with extra olives as soon as possible."

"Okay."

156

He took a couple of steps away from her, but stopped when she called out softly to him. "And, Tony . . ."

He paused, waiting.

Pepper said, "I'm not a cheeseburger."

He flashed her a grin. "No. You are *not* a cheeseburger." He headed toward the bar, missing the sudden flush of color in her face.

Chapter Eighteen

Inside, Tony made his way to the bar, threading through dozens of people dancing and mingling. He ordered another glass of wine and the super-dry, olive-laden martini, and turned to go back to Pepper when he found himself face-to-face with Christine, the reporter he had met months earlier. Suddenly he wished he could remember her last name.

"Mr. Stark!" she said brightly. "I was hoping I could get a reaction from you."

Candidly, Tony asked, "How's 'panic'?"

Christine's eyes got a little icier. "I was referring to your company's involvement in this latest atrocity."

Tony noticed she was holding something behind her, keeping it out of his sight. He knew it could be nothing good, but still he tried to put on a jovial face. "Hey, they just put my name on the invitations, y'know?"

Her expression not changing one iota, Christine thrust a dossier full of photos out to him. "Is this what you call accountability?"

Tony reluctantly placed both drinks on a passing waiter's tray and took the photos. After looking at only three or four, his face turned gray and his own expression locked down. "When were these taken?" he asked, his voice not completely steady.

"Yesterday." She all but sneered at him. "Good PR move—you tell the world you're a changed man. Even I believed you."

Tony couldn't believe what he was looking at: Afghan insurgents, the banner with ten rings emblazoned on their vehicles, triumphant in front of a burning, demolished town. Bodies lay strewn about, broken, mangled.

Every one of the insurgents held Stark Industries machine guns and grenade launchers.

Tony's hands trembled as he sifted through more of the photos. The scene changed: Now the shots were of civilians being force-marched in rows, with Stark weapons trained at their backs.

His voice hollow, Tony said, "I didn't approve this shipment."

"Well, your company did."

Tony looked her in the eye. "Come with me."

"I'm not going anywhere with you!"

Tony tried to think of a response, but found he was so angry he didn't trust himself. Instead he turned on his heel and walked away swiftly, headed for the main entrance—toward the people he needed desperately to address.

The paparazzi.

It took less than three seconds for the tide of camera flashes and shouted questions to turn and focus on Tony instead of on the latest arrival, and the tide surged when the reporters and photographers realized he actually *wanted* their attention. Cries of "What's going on, Mr. Stark?" and "You got something on your mind, Tony?" changed to silence when Tony raised his hands.

A pin could have been heard dropping on the red carpet.

"I made some promises I'm not going to be able to keep," Tony said, letting his voice carry. "Please help me get the word out on this. I suggest all of you pull all your money out of Stark Industries immediately—"

The crowd exploded in a roar of questions, the flashbulbs creating a blinding glare, and suddenly Obadiah appeared, steering Tony forcefully up toward the entrance stairs. Tony allowed himself to be steered, smiling. He felt good, having said only as much as he had, and he intended to tell the crowd much more.

Obadiah sounded miserable. "Is this like a tic for you? Whenever you have a feeling, you start going to all the people who don't trust you, who don't protect you. They're going to put a spin on everything you say!"

"Wait a minute," Tony said soberly. "I have to ask you something. I'm dead serious about this. Am I losing my mind or is Pepper really cute? Do you think she's attractive and interesting, or is it just that her hair is down? I've been out of the game for a while."

Obadiah's irritation cranked up several notches. "Are you out of your *mind*? You're messing with the 'guys in the rooms,' we're talking about billion-dollar interests, the *world order—*"

Tony waved one hand dismissively. "I'm not worried about that right now."

"Well, you *should be!* Tony, you'll disappear. I can't protect you against people like that."

The throng of paparazzi had been edging closer and closer, and now the floodgates opened again, with photo after photo snapped of the two of them arguing.

Obadiah turned to them and bellowed, *"Do you mind?"* He took Tony's elbow and pulled him higher up on the steps. His voice lowered again, Obadiah hissed, "Don't be so naive."

Tony's smile finally faded. "Naive? I was naive before, when I was growing up and they told me, 'Don't ever cross this line, this is how we do business.' In the meantime we're double-dealing under the table. We don't even deserve to represent the United States."

Obadiah scoffed. "Tony, you're a *child*!"

Tony's brow furrowed. "You don't believe I can turn this company around, do you?"

"You've got about as much control over things as a child riding in the backseat of his father's car with a red plastic steering wheel in his hand."

Tony shrugged. "Maybe I'll just get out of the car."

Obadiah's face changed. As Tony watched, the protective, well-meaning, Uncle-Obadiah demeanor dissolved and vanished, and Tony took a step backward, away from this man he suddenly realized he didn't know at all. It was as if someone new had stepped inside Obadiah Stane's skin and now glared at him with hate-filled eyes.

"You're not even allowed in the car," Obadiah barked. "*I'm* the one who filed the injunction against you."

It took several seconds for that to sink in. When it finally did, Tony suddenly felt very small and very much alone. In that moment he forgot where he was, he almost forgot *who* he was. He only knew that he had been betrayed by someone in whom he had always put every last shred of his trust.

Obadiah backed away, still glaring at Tony. "It's the only way I could protect you!" Obadiah shouted, but Tony knew those words were meant more for the reporters than for him.

He had no chance to take the confrontation further, though, as several large men in suits—all of them smiling but steely-eyed—moved to intercept Tony as Obadiah marched past the crowd toward a waiting car. Tony knew these men; they were all Stark Industries employees, and he considered telling them to get the hell out of his way. But then he realized who they truly were.

Obadiah's men.

Powerless to do anything else, Tony shouted after Obadiah, "This is going to stop!"

Obadiah got into the car and slammed the door, punctuating the scene. Deflated, Tony watched him go. Then he turned and wandered off into the darkness, away from the concert hall, away from everyone.

Chapter Nineteen

Tony left the fund-raiser and retreated to the safety of his workshop. Not to hide: to prepare.

Not once did it cross his mind that he had left Pepper standing on the veranda. Tony's thoughts focused solely on the task in front of him. He stood in the center of the lab again, the gleaming-red metal gauntlet on his right hand wired to the Repulsor unit in his chest. He made adjustments to the gauntlet's power level with a tiny screwdriver.

On the wall nearby, the flat-screen TV displayed live footage of a war-torn Middle Eastern country. Terrified groups of tattered refugees huddled in the filth-covered streets of bombed-out villages, homeless and miserable. Across the bottom of the screen crawled the words, "TRAGEDY IN GULMIRA." Tony glanced at the screen, listening as he continued work on the gauntlet.

"The ten-mile drive to the outskirts of Gulmira can only be described as a descent into hell, into a modern-day heart of darkness," the reporter's voiceover said.

"Simple farmers and herders from peaceful villages, driven from their homes by the butt of Western rifles and the turrets of modern tanks. Displaced from their lands by warlords and insurgent groups emboldened by their newfound power—a power fueled by high-tech weapons easily purchased with poppy money on the black market—and further destabilizing a fragile region which for decades has been a tinderbox of tribal feuding and ethnic hatred."

Tony finished the adjustment and stuck the little screwdriver into his back pocket. Then he held out his arm and raised his hand, so that the glowing blue Repulsor outlet in the gauntlet's palm aimed directly at a light fixture on the ceiling halfway down the length of the workshop. Tony triggered a Repulsor blast.

The light fixture sparked madly and crashed to the floor, its anchor strut sheared through.

The reporter's voice continued. "The villagers have taken shelter in whatever crude dwellings they can find—in the ruins of other razed villages, in the cold barren scrublands, or in the remnants of an old Soviet smelting plant. Our translator relayed to us one human tragedy after another. A seven-year-old boy, thin as a scarecrow, clutching yellowed photographs and holding them out to anyone who would stop, with a child's simple question: 'Where are my mother and father?' A woman, begging for news of her husband, who'd been kidnapped by insurgents."

While the reporter spoke, Tony pulled the screwdriver back out and made another adjustment. He fired a Repulsor blast the length of the workshop and into the garage, where it shattered another car window.

Tony frowned at the television as the reporter kept talking. "With no political will or international pressure, there is little hope for these newly formed refugees. Refugees who can only wonder one thing: Is the world watching?"

Tony was about to turn away from the screen, when he caught a glimpse of something that made him suck in a surprised breath. "Jarvis! Rewind that fifteen seconds and then play in slow motion."

"With pleasure, sir."

The newscast wound backward and played, slowly, so that Tony got a good look this time. Far in the background, beyond the destruction of the village, a flatbed truck flashed across the screen. And mounted on its bed was the unmistakable outline of a Jericho missile.

Tony raised the gauntlet and blasted a hole through the plasma-screen. The act held a measure of finality, as if both the physical and mental preparations for some unknown task had just been completed. Tony lowered his arm, staring at the screen. Then he unhooked the wire from the Repulsor unit and pulled the gauntlet off.

Tony was standing at the main workbench, deep in thought, when the door opened and Pepper walked in, clearly having come straight from the fund-raiser. Her splendid, professionally applied makeup had dimmed a bit, and she had shoved her hair into a hasty updo, but her gown remained magnificent.

Some part of Tony's mind sincerely wished he could appreciate the way she looked right now.

Pepper had come in prepared to read Tony the riot act; she had stood on that veranda for a solid hour, waiting for him to come back, and felt like an utter fool when someone told her he had left.

But now, standing in the workshop, looking around at all the destruction—especially the huge hole in the ceiling—Pepper started to understand that much more was developing here than simple inconsiderate behavior.

"Tony," she began, "are you going to tell me what's going on?"

He didn't look at her. Didn't even turn around. He just said, "Get my house in Dubai ready. I want to throw a party."

He could have been talking to a parking attendant for all the passion in his voice. Pepper floundered for a second, flustered by his brusqueness and then angered by it, before she composed herself. "Yes," she said, her own tone chilly, "Mr. Stark."

He made no response.

She turned and left him there, her jaw clenched.

Sunset.

The glittering lights of Dubai City began to come on, a slow, radiant swell that lit the bustling, modern metropolis from one end to the other and twinkled from the towering glass of its skyscrapers. A high-tech, tourist-friendly jewel nestled on the bank of the Persian Gulf, mere hours' travel from a sea of trackless, barren dunes, Dubai City attracted the wealthiest and most powerful of the global business elite.

Tony Stark was no different, in that the villa he maintained on the outskirts of the city doubled as luxury getaway and horrendously ostentatious status symbol. The sixteen-bedroom mansion overlooked the Gulf, and boasted an enormous custom swimming pool in the backyard.

The party had already gotten under way, but the rhythm of the crowd picked up as the sun finally disappeared. The partygoers, to a person, could have been described as "the beautiful people." No military top brass, no A-list celebrities, just phenomenally gorgeous, phenomenally wealthy women and men, with more arriving by expensive cars every minute. Valets scurried to keep up with the flow.

Inside the house, Tony wove through the crowd, a glass of $700 champagne in his hand. He greeted his guests, shook hands, slapped shoulders. A man in his forties who came from a family soaking in old money called out to him.

"Tony! You never said, what is the big occasion?"

Tony winked at him. "Ever known me to need one?"

The man laughed heartily. Tony moved past him, smiling as he circulated.

• • •

Hours later, the party had shifted its center of gravity to the pool, where the guests drank and danced at poolside or splashed around in the water. Tony wandered through the crowd, two dark-skinned, exotic beauties on his arms. He knew their names were Aysha and Inaya. He just couldn't remember who was who.

Inaya—or maybe Aysha—had leaned close to him and begun to nibble on his earlobe when Tony noticed Pepper making her way toward him. Pepper's hair and clothes had returned to what he couldn't help but think of as "normal," which was to say "really conservative" and "sort of severe." The crowd gave her a wide berth.

Pepper's voice remained neutral as she stopped in front of Tony and said, "Well, you seem to be back in old form."

Tony grinned at her. "Life of the party—isn't that what everyone wanted?" He shifted the grin to one of the women. "Cue the fireworks in five, would you, Pepper?"

Tony turned the women and stumbled toward the house with them.

Pepper hadn't moved. She stared holes in Tony's back as he left. "Sure," she said, her words hard-edged. "Don't hurt yourself."

Tony entered the house with Aysha and Inaya, climbed unsteadily to the second floor, and shoved open the door to his bedroom. Both of them giggling now, the two women tumbled onto the huge bed.

Tony followed them in, but stopped in the middle of the floor, watching them with a smile. "I'll be right back," he told them.

The women laughed while Tony checked his watch. He crossed to a side door and slipped out through it. As the door closed behind him, he straightened up and strode purposefully down a hallway, the women already forgotten.

Two minutes later, back out at the pool, the party guests gathered together to "ooh" and "aah" as a massive fireworks display erupted from the other side of the house. Rockets hissed and boomed as they arced into the night sky and exploded into spectacular displays of red, green, white, and intense blue.

Pepper stood apart from the crowd. She watched the show, but felt in no way festive. She frowned faintly and wondered how she had allowed herself to become so miserable.

Another round of rockets went up, and Pepper noted dully that a brilliant blue one didn't detonate, but instead arced out over the ocean and disappeared.

She figured it was a dud and gave it no further thought.

Chapter Twenty

Smoke and dust obscured the light of the following morning's sunrise as gunfire and the dull explosions of grenades filled the air.

Black-clad insurgent soldiers prowled through the sprawling, decayed husk of an abandoned industrial complex, weapons in their hands, on the hunt. The huge factory, defunct for better than two decades, had until this morning played host to hundreds of Gulmiran refugees. Most of the open spaces in and around the now empty central building were filled with tents and shanties.

The refugees had scattered at the soldiers' arrival. Now they hid and scurried among the wreckage like the tiniest of field mice, terrified, knowing that if any of the hunters found them it meant certain death.

The soldiers swept through the complex, tossing grenades down "rat holes" where they suspected refugees to be, firing at anything that moved and worrying later about what they hit.

At one side of the central building, a mother and her four children pressed as far back as they could against the rear wall of a cavelike crawl space in the building's foundation. The mother tried to wrap her arms around every child, but she didn't have enough arms to cover them all.

From outside came the sound of high-pitched, yelping barks, barely audible through the gunfire.

The oldest of the children jerked his head up to look his mother in the eye. "Arto's out there!" he whispered.

She gasped and grabbed him around the upper arm. "Don't you *dare*!" she hissed back. "You stay right here, young man! Don't you dare move a *muscle*!"

The boy stayed still . . . for the ten seconds until he heard the dog's bark again. Then, breaking free of his mother's grip, he scrambled forward and darted out of the crawl space into the alley beside the next building.

He spotted the puppy instantly. Tiny, brown, roly-poly, the little dog's tail normally wagged like an unstoppable metronome. Now the pup pressed itself against a ruined brick wall, tail between its legs, crying and yelping and calling out for help from its master.

The boy called out again, "Arto!" and dashed toward the dog, scooping him up into his arms. The boy turned to make his way back to the crawl space, puppy safely in tow and found himself staring at four men with rifles in their hands. Two of them grinned.

"Drop the dog, little man," one of the soldiers shouted. "Drop it. Right now."

The boy shook his head reluctantly; he knew what was about to happen to him. But he wouldn't, he *couldn't*, let Arto be abandoned like that. He couldn't bear the thought of Arto left alone again, miserable and crying. "N-no," he said quietly. Then louder: "No!"

Now three of the men smiled. All four of them raised their weapons, sighted on the boy . . . and something like a meteor flashed out of the sky and slammed into the ground in front of the soldiers. The boy's mouth dropped open in amazement. It was a man made of red-and-gold metal, and where the metal man's fist smashed the earth, the ground itself shook and cracked.

The soldiers didn't have the chance to fire even one bullet. The metal man stood and held up his hands, and a wave of blue light shot out of the palms and swatted the four soldiers away as if they'd been struck by a gigantic baseball bat. They landed in heaps and didn't get back up.

The metal man turned, grabbed the boy and the yelping puppy, and lifted off the ground again, speeding them down the length of the alleyway to stop right in front of the crawl space where the rest of the boy's family hid. The boy gawked at the blue radiance thrumming from his rescuer's feet.

The metal man set the boy down with the puppy still in his arms. The boy's mother rushed out from the back of the alcove and wrapped her arms around her son, laughing and weeping at the same time.

The bottoms of the metal man's boots glowed brilliant blue again. He lifted off, angled sideways, and rocketed back toward the soldiers like a missile.

Ignoring his mother's protests, the boy broke free of her grip and ran to the crawl-space entrance again to look for any sign of the metal man who'd saved his life. What he saw was a black-clad soldier fly out from behind a huge pile of bricks, limp as a rag-doll, and crash headlong to the ground.

He crept out, just a few more paces, just enough to get a good look—and there he was again! The metal man stood in the center of what must have been thirty soldiers, all of them attacking him, shooting their guns at him, firing enough shots to kill a whole army.

But the metal man shrugged off the gunshots as if they were no more than buzzing gnats. He swung his fists, knocking the soldiers back, slamming them flat to the ground. That might have been enough if there had been fewer men. But they kept coming, and the boy's eyes got huge.

The metal man lifted his hand and pointed his palm toward a group of soldiers, and a flash of blue light smashed them off their feet. The combination of fists and strange blue flares proved too much for the soldiers. They turned and ran, and some of them even threw down their useless weapons as they went.

As the men in black fled, panicked, through the streets, little by little the refugees began to poke their heads out from hiding, watching in wonder.

A little girl came to stand next to the boy. "What

is happening?" she asked. "Why are they running?"

The boy pointed at the metal man, who stood, triumphant, watching the soldiers go.

Then the metal man's head turned as he pinpointed a new group of men, bearing down on him from another alleyway. He rocketed away to meet the new threat on a pillar of blue electric flame.

On the other side of the industrial complex, in a small building that had once served as the payroll office, Raza watched through a pair of binoculars as a column of his men came barreling out from one of the alleys, fleeing in terror.

Raza swore, grabbed a rifle, and stomped through his small command post toward the exit, shouldering aside a couple of his aides along the way. He paused in the doorway and looked through the binoculars again to get his bearings. From this new angle, he got a crystal-clear view of the man in the red-and-gold armor throwing one of his soldiers through a wall.

Raza froze in his tracks and watched, riveted.

Down in the middle of the complex, bullets still pinging and ricocheting off his armor, Tony spotted a soldier about to fire an RPG at him. The soldier hesitated for one second too long, though, and Tony reached him, picked him up by his collar, and held a palm up to the man's face. The Repulsor emitter glowed and hummed with power.

The soldier had seen more than enough of what that

Repulsor could do, and through gray, bloodless lips he screamed, "Geneva Convention! Article Three! Geneva Convention!"

Tony growled, crushed the man's rifle with his free hand, and tossed the soldier aside as if throwing away garbage. The man scrambled to his feet and ran for his life.

Tony swiveled his head, looking for a new target. There was one very specific thing he was looking for here, and he hadn't found it yet.

He both heard and felt something strike him between the shoulder blades with a resounding *clang*. The sniper's bullet hadn't penetrated his armor, hadn't even come close, but the impact still jarred him enough to get his undivided attention.

Tony made a best guess at what direction the shot must have come from, faced that way, and triggered the thermal imaging array in his HUD. Instantly the complex around him rendered itself in vivid shades of red, green, yellow, and gray, the colors fading and varying depending on the temperature of the object they represented.

There: on top of a three-story building a few hundred yards away. Tony spotted the bright-red silhouette of a sniper and immediately fired a Repulsor burst, but across the bottom of the HUD flashed the words "OUT OF RANGE."

Clang. The sniper hit him again. The impact still didn't penetrate the armor, but it did knock him off-balance for a second. Tony looked around, improvising.

He knew that a basic rule of snipers was never to fire from the same location twice if you could help it. You never wanted the enemy to know where you were, not only because the element of surprise was the sniper's best friend, but also because the enemy would inevitably hunt you down and kill you if they could find you.

The man who kept shooting at him was either a very bad sniper or very stupid, because he made no attempt to move. Tony saw him jack another shell into the chamber of his rifle, just as the perfect impromptu weapon presented itself.

Tony moved quickly over to a discarded tire, shreds of rubber still clinging to the rim. He picked it up easily with one hand. Calculations cascaded across his HUD, sensors taking into account everything from distance to wind speed and direction, and as they finished, the on-board system drew a hyperbolic arc on the display leading straight to the sniper.

Tony drew back his arm and flung the tire as if it were a discus.

The impact knocked the sniper off the roof and Tony marked the fall with the thermal array, watching the flailing red shape as it plummeted to the ground below. Tony turned, scanning the rest of the complex, and saw at least three dozen more red shapes stalking him.

He rose a few feet in the air and powered up the Repulsors in his gauntlets, ready to take them on.

• • •

Bright, hard sunlight shone down on Gulmira as Tony tore into Raza's soldiers, but at that moment stars flickered above the Central Air Operations Center at Edwards Air Force Base. The late hour didn't matter to Major Gregory Allen, a thickset, craggy man in his fifties, as he pushed his way into the CAOC and looked around.

The monitor room was never brightly lit, but tonight it seemed unusually dim. The fifteen officers on monitor duty seemed more like cave trolls than soldiers, all of them hunched at their stations, staring at the same grainy images. The only light came from the banks of monitors and the huge observation screens that displayed those images. Major Allen squinted and tried to make sense out of what he was seeing.

A USAF satellite piped in a live feed: something moved in an abandoned industrial site, a place Intelligence had already noted as a shoddy refugee camp. Scores of insurgents crowded around the thing, trying to take it down and failing miserably. The thing, whatever it was, moved among them, knocking the men about like tenpins and every so often flattening a group of them with some kind of flash of light.

Through the haze and the graininess and the smoke, Allen got a brief glimpse of the cause of all the destruction. He took a short, sharp breath, causing one of the officers to glance up at him.

The major scowled. "Are we in there?"

"Negative, sir," the officer replied. "It's a local skirmish, green-on-green."

Allen flicked his eyes from one screen to the next, hoping to get another clear picture. "Anyone want to tell me what I'm looking at?"

The same officer answered. "A drone? An advanced robotic? We don't know what it is, sir."

Allen's scowl deepened. "Get someone down here from Weapons Development. *Now.*"

The blasted, burned-out complex that so many refugees had been forced to call home had fallen eerily silent.

Tony took advantage of the lull to check his readouts: power at 97 percent and climbing, armor integrity not damaged at all. The Mark III suit functioned perfectly.

He turned in a slow circle, looking at all the refugees who had begun to emerge from their holes and venture out into the daylight. Tony lifted his arms in what he hoped was a peaceful gesture, and would have liked to have said something, but he hadn't had the time or the forethought to install any language translation software.

"My Gulmiran is a little rusty," he said anyway, on the chance someone here might speak English. "But I want you to know I'm here to help you. I—"

His sentence was cut short by a fiery explosion that destroyed the building immediately to his left.

As the refugees scattered again, Tony had just enough presence of mind to think, *That sounded like one of mine.* Then a second detonation went off much closer,

178

knocking him off-balance so severely that he tipped and fell like an axed tree.

A huge, matte-black Stark Industries tank burst straight through one of the village's huts and sped toward him, its turret swiveling, the wide-mouthed gun zeroing in on him and ready to fire again. Tony got to his feet and faced off against the machine.

He knew from memory that the tank would need at least 1.8 more seconds to fire another shell. That gave him time to load the tank's schematics from his on-board database into his heads-up display. A laserlike grid overlaid the tank, paused for half a second, and highlighted a tiny maintenance port on the rear of the machine just below the base of the turret.

Tony raised one arm. A hatch lifted and slid aside on the forearm, revealing a mini-missile pod.

Tony locked the missile's targeting system onto the tank's weak spot and fired.

The projectile took off on a wide curve, accelerated so quickly that it made its own tiny sonic boom, and slammed straight into the maintenance port.

The initial explosion sounded minor, but it was followed immediately by another from inside the tank, then another as the entire tank blew apart, practically disintegrating. Tiny scraps of debris rained down over a wide area as Tony scanned again. This time he saw no more stealth movement . . . but he did pick up motion directly behind him and whirled, Repulsor charged and ready to fire, only to see the little boy he had scooped up and carried to safety minutes before. The kid grinned at him and held out an apple.

Tony mussed the boy's hair gently. "Hey, you keep the apple, kid," he said, his voice tender. "But I appreciate the thought." Then he took a few steps away, powered up the propulsion boots, and blasted off. He still hadn't found what he'd come for. Maybe he would now that things had quieted down a little.

Tony let the thermal imaging spread out as he rose in altitude until it encompassed the whole complex.

Nothing.

It had to be here somewhere.

He started flying ever-increasing circles around the complex, scanning, concentrating—*there*!

He would never have seen it without the thermal display. Still on the back of the flatbed, camouflaged under a thick screen of debris, was the Jericho missile Tony had spotted on the newscast. Half a mile from the complex, easily far enough away to prevent any civilians from getting hurt.

It took less than a second to lock onto the target. The gauntlet-mounted mini-missile launcher deployed once more, and the tiny projectile sped away, again creating its own sonic boom as it ripped through the air.

Tony grinned as the mini-missile struck home and the Jericho disappeared in a blazing plume of fire.

Unseen by anyone, Raza crouched nearby in the cramped space directly beneath one building's roof, peering out through a gap in the bricks as the man in red and gold cruised back through the complex, flying below rafter-height.

Raza pulled a satellite phone out of a pouch at his belt and dialed a number. When the other end answered, he said, "Put me through to the boss."

Chapter Twenty-one

Outside, the refugees gathered in a ragged but hopeful group and cheered heartily as Tony flew one more pass over them. Tony waved, then banked sharply and climbed up into the clouds.

Behind the faceplate, he allowed himself a satisfied grin. "Jarvis, plot a course for home."

"Very good, sir," Jarvis answered, and registered no complaints at all about Tony's performance.

The armor flashed its brilliant colors in the sun as Tony arced leisurely away.

At the Central Air Operations Center, though, leisure was nowhere to be found. Lieutenant Colonel James Rhodes burst through the doors, pulling off his jacket, and stared hard at the images of the Gulmira assault as he stalked past the screens. He stopped in front of the largest one, his eyes fixed on it.

"So what do we have here, Rhodes?" Major Allen asked from the back of the room.

"I don't think it's Russian or Chinese," Rhodey answered without hesitation.

"Then where did it come from?"

That gave Rhodey pause. He thought hard for a few moments and finally said, "Let me make a call." Rhodey stepped over to a control console nestled between two of the larger screens and punched in a number.

Seconds later, 15,000 feet over the Persian Gulf, glowing yellow words flashed on Tony's heads-up display: DOD EMERGENCY CALL.

"Sir," Jarvis said with only the tiniest note of alarm, "the Department of Defense seems to be on the phone."

Not entirely sure what to make of this, Tony said, "Put it through, Jarvis." He waited for the line to connect, then said, "Yeah?"

In the controlled chaos of the CAOC, Rhodey paced, holding a handset with a long cord attached to the control console he'd dialed from. He tried to stay as far away as possible from anyone who might overhear him. That wasn't easy, as officers darted to and fro around him and a constant, growing murmur of activity filled the room.

"Tony, it's Rhodey." He paused, frustrated. "What is that noise?"

"I'm in the convertible," said Tony's voice over the phone. "This isn't really the best time."

"I need a quick ID. What do you know about unmanned combat robotics, with air-ground capabilities?"

"Never heard of anything like that. Why?"

Rhodey heard Major Allen and one of the other officers talking softly and looked over his shoulder. Both men were watching a monitor that displayed a political map, on which the unknown robotic's flight path showed up as a red dot moving west. The dot was just about to cross a bright green border and as soon as it did, another officer spoke up. "Unmanned Aerial Vehicle has entered the no-fly zone."

"Because I think I'm staring at one right now," Rhodey said. "And it's about to get blown up."

Alarms went off in the CAOC as Major Allen gave the intercept order. "Rhodes!" The major shouted from across the room. "You got something for me, or not?"

Over the phone, Tony said, "Uhh . . . 'blown up?'"

Ten miles south of Tony's position, two USAF F-22 Raptor fighter jets flashed out of a cloud bank like a pair of sharks and powered north, homed in on the target indicator flashing red on their screens.

Immediately an alarm sounded inside Tony's helmet, and "PROXIMITY WARNING" flashed across the HUD in blood-red letters.

"This is my exit," Tony said into the phone, talking loudly enough to drown out most of the alarm sound. "Gotta go!" He broke the connection and triggered his own turbos, rolling in a tight bank and trying to zigzag.

Behind him, the two Raptors dropped down out of the sky and curved expertly onto his tail.

Standing in the CAOC, Major Allen and Rhodey watched the big screen as the two green blips followed the red one. "Ballroom Control, this is Viper One and Two checking in," one of the pilots said over the radio. "UAV is in sight."

The major didn't blink. "Viper: target at 330 for ten miles."

Another screen went blank, then lit up and split in half with images loading in directly from the belly-cams of the F-22s. Both planes were locked onto the fleeing red-and-gold mystery object, but neither one could catch it.

The object banked sharply, and there on the monitor, in full, clear color, everyone in the room got a good, solid look at what the jets were chasing. A few people gasped. Someone whistled.

Rhodey couldn't believe what he was seeing. "What is that thing?" he whispered to no one.

In the cockpit of one of the fighter jets, the pilot wrestled with the stick as he struggled to stay with the rocketlike object in front of him. The bogey shifted left and right in a zigzag that had the pilot's teeth rattling.

"Ballroom," he said through gritted teeth, "contact appears to be an unmanned aerial vehicle."

"Ballroom copies," Major Allen said over the radio. "You are cleared to engage."

The pilot fought the stick again, struggling to stay on the bogey's tail and to stay off his wingman. He banked hard to the left, describing an almost complete circle, and knew that just a few seconds more of this would be too much for him.

Then the automated voiced targeting system spoke up: "Locked on! Locked on!"

The pilot flipped off the cover of his thumb switch and hit it, firing one of the Raptor's sidewinder missiles.

Tony risked a glance over his shoulder as he screamed through the sky. The two jets were still there, of course, as he knew they would be, but—

"Oh no," Tony whispered, recognizing the white-hot, rapidly closing sidewinder at the exact moment that another alarm went off in his helmet. A bright red dot appeared on his HUD, zooming toward the center from the display's outer edge, and Jarvis announced, "Incoming sidewinder in five . . . four . . . three . . . two . . ."

"COUNTERMEASURES" flashed in yellow across the HUD as a hatch popped open on the suit's back. A loose ball of chaff flew out, the long, wide metallic strips beginning to expand, and when the blast from the propulsion boots hit it, the ball exploded into a broad cloud of fluttering, floating debris.

The sidewinder flew straight into the cloud, which

it registered as a solid object, and blew up with a sound like a volcano erupting. A massive ball of flame expanded from the point of detonation, engulfing Tony, but a tenth of a second later he came rocketing out of it, still in control, still pouring on the speed.

Both Raptors veered away from the fireball, but came right back onto the target as if they were on rails. Tony went into a power-dive, blasting straight down for a solid mile, then pulled a nearly 90-degree turn as he tried to shake the fighter jets loose.

In one corner of Tony's HUD, a small meter labeled "G-FORCE" sprang to life and immediately shot into the red. Tony fought to keep his eyes open as all the blood drained from his head and he nearly passed out from gravitational strain.

"Sir," Jarvis said reproachfully, "may I remind you that while the suit can handle these maneuvers, *you* cannot?"

Before Tony had a chance to answer, both the F-22s opened fire with heavy cannons, and the air around him seemed to ignite as countless tracer rounds streaked past. Then the Raptors corrected their targeting errors and the rounds started hitting him directly, pounding him, exploding on contact. Tony faltered and flailed in midair, and Jarvis said, "Sir, the suit cannot take a sustained amount of this punishment."

"I'm well aware of that, Jarvis!" Tony shouted. "*Air brakes!*"

Flaps popped out along the length of Tony's arms and legs, and down the side seam of his torso. He immediately dropped to one-quarter speed and watched as both fighter jets blew past him.

The pilot that Major Allen addressed as "Viper One" looked behind him, blinked his eyes rapidly, and looked behind him again. His wingman spoke into his ear. "You ever seen *anything* do that before?"

Viper One shook his head slowly. It took him a moment to find any words. "That . . . was *not* a drone." He checked his scope, preparing to turn around and reacquire the target, but the scope showed nothing.

Aside from the two Raptors, the sky was empty.

The second pilot had the same results. Over the radio he demanded, "Where is it?"

The jets widened into a broad circular search pattern but found nothing.

Standing in the middle of the CAOC monitor room, Rhodey stared at the two feeds from the Raptors' belly cams. The longer he thought about it, the likelier a certain set of circumstances seemed and the more Rhodey's stomach sank at the thought.

When one of the tech officers said, "Lieutenant Colonel Rhodes, I have Tony Stark calling," Rhodey knew his instincts were correct.

"Put him through." He picked up the handset he'd used earlier, frowning as a low roaring noise filled his ear.

"Rhodey, I had Jarvis run a check," Tony said at the other end of the line. He practically had to shout to make himself heard. "I might have some info on that UAV. A piece of gear like that might exist. Might *definitely exist . . .*"

Rhodey squeezed his eyes shut and spoke in as low a voice as he could, trying not to envision his best friend up on charges for the unauthorized deploying of an advanced drone into a foreign country. "Wouldn't happen to be red and gold, would it?"

As Tony and Rhodey spoke on the phone, the two Raptors continued their wide-circle search pattern. "The thing has to be here," Viper One muttered. "It couldn't have just—"

Before he could say the word *disappeared*, Viper One glanced out toward Viper Two, which had begun a slow bank to the right. He found himself staring straight at the red-and-gold bogey, clinging to the underside of his partner's plane.

"Viper Two—he's on your belly!" the pilot shouted. "Shake him!"

Major Allen's eyes bugged out of his head as he stared at the feed from Viper One's belly cam. Viper Two shuddered and rolled in a valiant attempt to dislodge the metallic stowaway, but the red-and-gold figure hung on for dear life.

Viper One's voice piped in over the room's speakers. "Ballroom: that is definitely *not* a UAV."

The major couldn't take his eyes off the monitor. "What is it, then?"

"Sir, I—I think it's a *man*. Sir."

Rhodey's face lost all color as the last piece clicked into place, and he whispered, "Son of a—"

Then, into the handset, he shouted, "Tony!"

But the line was dead.

In his cockpit, the Viper Two pilot looked frantically out one side, then the other, desperate to see the unexplained *thing* attached to his aircraft. Viper One's voice blasted out of the radio: "Still there, Viper Two! Roll! Roll!"

Viper Two wrenched his stick to the left, sending his F-22 into a tight corkscrew. "Let go!" he shouted, not even realizing it. *"Let go!"*

Tony felt as if he was stuck inside a centrifuge as the sky and the land rolled and spun crazily around him. The alarm still went off in his helmet, joined now by a couple of buzzers and a flashing red light. Front and center on the HUD was the message: "POWER 28%."

Jarvis's voice somehow cut through the din. "Sir. Two minutes and there won't be sufficient power to get home."

"Two more minutes of this," Tony grunted, "and my skull's going to cave in." He tightened his grip on the F-22's hull, used it for leverage, and thrust himself away from the jet as forcefully as he could.

The plane Tony had been clinging to fell away, mercifully clear, and Tony was about to try to ignite his propulsion boots when his entire field of vision filled with the onrushing mass of the first Raptor. He had no time to speak or even react before he hit the fighter jet's tail fin straight-on and sheared it completely off the plane.

Tony and the F-22 both spiraled out of control, spinning away from each other at deadly speeds.

Chapter Twenty-two

"I'm hit!" Viper One screamed, and yanked the EJECT lever. Explosive bolts blasted the canopy clear, and he followed it less than a second afterward. He knew to hold steady, that the parachute would open automatically when he had reached a safe distance from the plane.

But it didn't open.

The pilot gasped and shut his eyes, trying to block out the madly spinning world around him, but opened them again as he groped for the emergency parachute release. He found the lever, tugged on it, and discovered it had been damaged, either in the collision with the bogey or during the ejection.

Viper One couldn't hear Major Allen's voice over the radio, shouting at his wingman: "Viper Two, do you see a chute?"

"Negative! No chute, no chute!"

Viper One simply watched, helpless, as he plummeted toward the earth, the horizon and the sky whirling around him.

• • •

High above the collision site, just as the Raptor pilot's ejection seat blew free of the wrecked plane, Tony sped through the clouds, waiting for his head to stop spinning and throbbing. "Power *critical*," Jarvis said into his ear. "Set course for home immediately."

But Tony couldn't help looking down, just to make sure the pilot made it out safely. He realized in an instant that the F-22 below him was in trouble, and without hesitation Tony dropped into another power-dive. Tendrils of water vapor twisted into vortices in the wake of his propulsion boots, as he tore out of the cloud and screamed downward, on a collision course with the falling aircraft.

The second fighter jet had arced back around, but Tony didn't let himself think about that. He caught up with the first plane, matched his speed—and for a moment, he and the pilot were face-to-face, staring at each other as the wind whipped past them.

Tony grabbed the damaged rip cord, popped it free of the kink in the metal that had kept it in place, and released the pilot's parachute.

The chute snapped open, deploying perfectly, and yanked the pilot up and away.

Tony breathed a sigh of relief that got crunched into a curse, as he realized that the ground was *right there*—another second and he'd plow straight into it. He spun and pointed his boots downward and let loose ferocious twin streams of Repulsor fire from his gauntlets, trying to pull up, trying to turn . . . and turn he did, avoiding the ground by less than three feet.

Tony climbed back up to a safe altitude, trying to figure out which way was home, and cursed again when the second F-22 barrel-rolled onto his tail.

Seconds earlier, Viper Two's transmission had filled the CAOC monitor room: "Good chute! Good chute! You're not gonna believe this, Ballroom, but that thing just saved Viper One!"

Major Allen and Rhodey stood side by side now, both of them staring unblinkingly at the central screen, which was filled with the feed from Viper Two's belly cam. Both of them had witnessed the bogey's spectacular dive, as well as the release of the damaged chute.

The major hesitated for less than two seconds. "Viper Two: re-engage."

Rhodey whipped his head around. *"What?"*

"Take the target out!" the major shouted, his face turning red.

"Major, call off that Raptor!" Rhodey all but shouted himself. "You don't know what you're shooting at!"

Allen grimaced, determined. "We'll find out when we recover the pieces."

The two of them heard the targeting system in Viper Two's cockpit activate, as the feminine voice announced, "Locked on! Locked on!"

Viper Two's voice came through tentatively.

"Ballroom: understand, you want me to engage the UAV?"

"Copy," Allen snapped.

"Negative!" Rhodey took a step toward the screen in an unconscious effort to make himself heard. "Viper Two, *disengage!*"

"It's not your call!" Allen shouted at him. "That thing just took out an F-22 inside a legal no-fly zone!" The major turned his attention to the screen again. "Viper Two: You get a clean shot, you take it!"

"And then you can explain to Viper One why you blasted the man who saved his life out of the sky," Rhodey all but snarled, and Allen took a step backward, his face paling. Rhodey turned back to the screen. "Disengage, Viper Two," he said loudly and clearly. "I say again, disengage. Do not fire on the bogey."

"Roger that." Viper Two sounded audibly relieved as he peeled away from the red-and-gold target.

Rhodey turned back to face Major Allen, who stood trembling, white-faced, his teeth grinding together.

Rhodey walked out of the room, right past the major, and neither man said a word.

In Tony Stark's Dubai City villa, Pepper Potts sat on a tasteful love-seat in a small alcove near the front entrance. The alcove faced the door, and in Pepper's plan, she would be sitting there, prim and proper and subtly but unmistakably disapproving, when Tony came in.

Falling asleep wasn't in her plan, but then she hadn't expected Tony to be gone all night *and* most of the next day. Pepper sat, her head propped against the wall, her mouth open ever so slightly, her breaths deep and regular. She was too well-composed to snore, though she did make a small sound like *"snerk"* when something whooshed past the nearest window and startled her awake.

Pepper stood and called out, "Tony?"

A thump sounded from the living room a short distance down the hallway. Pepper glanced around, uncertain of what she'd just heard, and cautiously moved down the hallway. Again she called, "Tony?"

Pepper entered the living room and froze solid in her tracks. Her breath caught in her chest.

Tony sat in a huge chair, dressed in a suit of red-and-gold high-tech armor, and he looked like sheer hell. The armor itself was scarred, pitted, and smoking. Tony had pulled off the helmet, which now sat on the floor next to the chair, and though he held a drink in one gauntleted hand, he appeared to be very close to passing out. Blood trickled from his nose and his ears, and random scorchlike soot streaks marred his face.

Tony looked at Pepper with eyes that wouldn't stay focused. Weakly, shaking, he whispered, "Get me home."

In Gulmira, several hours' drive north and forty-five hundred feet higher than the abandoned factory complex Tony had recently cleared out, the desolate wasteland lay beneath a blanket of snow. Rather than concealing the landscape's less attractive features, the snow served to accentuate them, so that the mountainside camp to which Raza and his men had retreated seemed to exist in a bleak, hopeless limbo of white.

A few yurts stood here and there. Raza's men sat inside the circular, tentlike structures, licking their wounds. Two of the soldiers had partially pulled off their shirts, comparing the huge, vividly colored bruises that covered their entire torsos: Evidence of damage done by the blue beams that had shot from the metal-clad stranger's hands.

Someone watching the path that led up to the camp cried out, and the soldiers grabbed their guns and lined up in formation. They were expecting this visit.

Coming up the steep, rocky path was a train of black Suburbans. The big vehicles came to a stop in the middle of the camp and disgorged a dozen private security guards: large men in expensive civilian clothing, all of them with the cold, steely stare of former Special Forces.

Raza sauntered out of one of the yurts and approached the lead Suburban. He stood, arms folded, waiting, and watched as the rear door finally popped open and Obadiah Stane stepped out, surveying the camp around him with a dispassionate eye.

"Welcome," Raza said, and gestured toward the yurt from which he had emerged.

Obadiah stepped forward and openly examined the hideous scars on Raza's face.

"Compliments of Tony Stark," Raza said coldly.

Obadiah remained unfazed. "If you'd killed him when you were supposed to, you'd still have a face."

Raza didn't blink. "You paid us trinkets to kill a prince. An insult to me and to the man whose ring I wear."

Obadiah shot a quick glance at the ring on Raza's right hand. It bore the familiar device of the ten interlocking rings. "I think it's best we don't get him involved in this." He looked Raza in the eye and said, "I've come a long way to see this weapon. Show me."

Raza nodded. "Come. Leave your guards outside."

Raza turned and made his way back to his yurt. Obadiah followed, his footsteps crunching in the snow, and stepped through the doorway into the circular, brightly lit enclosure.

Obadiah paused, eyes huge, staring.

There before him in the yurt hung the reassembled gray armor Tony Stark had built in the cave in Afghanistan, suspended on wires. Every piece had been carefully put back exactly as it had been, or at least as close as Raza's men could get it.

Only after he had taken in the bizarre, patchwork majesty of the armor did Obadiah notice a table set up nearby, on which rested a teapot, two cups, a sheaf of onionskin papers, a light board, and a laptop computer that looked as if it had been dragged behind a truck for several miles.

Raza stood to one side, arms folded, gauging Obadiah's reaction to the armor. "Stark's escape bore unexpected fruit," he said quietly.

Obadiah's eyebrows slowly raised. "So *this* is how he did it."

"It was only a crude first effort. But he has perfected his design." Raza produced a handful of grainy surveillance photos, which he handed over to Obadiah.

There were twelve photographs, each one of the red-and-gold armored man plowing through Raza's forces at the abandoned factory complex in Gulmira. His eyes lifted from the images to the hanging suit of armor, and anyone watching would have understood that Obadiah Stane had seen the future.

He gestured with his chin toward the table. "What's this?"

"The inside of Tony Stark's mind," Raza said with audible satisfaction. "Look."

Raza moved to the table, turned on the light board, and arranged the onionskin sketches on it. One by one he placed them, as if fitting pieces into a jigsaw puzzle, and when he finished Obadiah found it difficult to suppress a grin.

The sketches fit together perfectly to form a suit of armor identical in almost every way to the one pictured in the surveillance photos. "He was planning ahead," Obadiah whispered.

Raza waved a hand at the sketches and the laptop. "Everything you will need to build this weapon."

Obadiah turned and slowly circled the armor, eyeing it critically as Raza sat at the table and poured a cup of tea.

"Stark has made a masterpiece of death," Raza said casually. "A man with a dozen of these could rule from the Pacific to the Ukraine. And you dream of Stark's throne. We have a common enemy." He fixed his eyes on the gray metal suit. "The Iron Man."

Obadiah had made his way all the way around the armor. He lifted a hand and poked a finger at the center of the chest plate, where there was nothing but a large, vacant hole.

Raza sipped at the cup of tea. Then he stood and faced Obadiah. "If we are back in business, I give you these designs as my gift. In turn, I hope you will repay me with a gift of iron soldiers."

Obadiah smiled. It was the kind of smile he had become famous for: the warm, easy, comforting smile of a man who wants only the best for everyone, who would always lend a sympathetic ear whenever anyone had a problem. He put his hands on Raza's shoulders as if to give him a hug filled with solidarity and brotherhood.

Then Obadiah spoke—in perfect Urdu. *"This . . . is the only gift you shall receive."*

Raza's face, which had relaxed when Obadiah smiled at him, grew odd. Rigid. Raza's eyes became unfocused. Confused, he tried to move, but his limbs refused to respond.

Blood began to run from his left ear.

Obadiah stepped away and showed Raza the small, black device in his right hand. "This is a sonic Taser," Obadiah said, and removed a pair of filtering earplugs from his own ears. He watched coldly as Raza crumpled to the floor of the yurt.

"Technology." Obadiah let his voice fill with scorn. "It's always been your Achilles heel. Don't worry, it'll wear off in fifteen minutes, but that's the least of your problems."

Obadiah crouched, grabbed Raza's hand, and yanked the ring off it. Then he stood and walked out of the yurt.

Outside, all of Raza's men were lined up, on their knees, in front of the row of black Suburbans. Obadiah's men stood behind them, machine guns pointed at the backs of the insurgents' heads. Obadiah caught the eye of his second-in-command on this trip and jerked a thumb back toward the yurt.

"Crate up that armor and the rest of it. I'll be in the truck, where it's warm." He made his way past the kneeling soldiers.

"And these men?"

Obadiah didn't look back. "Take care of them."

And as the machine-gun fire rattled out, echoing off the mountainside, he didn't flinch at all.

Chapter Twenty-three

The next afternoon, Agent Phil Coulson walked into his bland, unremarkable office, sat down, and picked up the phone. He hit a number that he had set to speed dial and leaned back in his chair as the phone rang.

When the other end answered, Coulson sat up and leaned forward, propping his elbows on the desktop. "Ms. Potts. It's Agent Coulson from the Strategic Homeland Inter—" He stopped and made a slight face as she cut him off.

"Yes, I know." Pepper Potts's voice sounded even more brusque on the phone than it had in person. "Unfortunately Tony is not going to be available to sit down with you for a while."

"Really?" Coulson asked. "And why is that?"

He frowned as, abruptly, Potts lost her calm, cool façade and began struggling for words. "He's, uh, there's a . . . Tony won't be—"

Coulson broke in on her this time, wondering if the two of them were ever going to let each other finish two sentences in a row. "Maybe I can meet with you instead?"

At that moment, standing in Tony Stark's living room, Pepper Potts furrowed her brow in puzzlement, though she did feel grateful for the diversion from Tony. "Me? Why? I don't know anything."

Then Pepper mentally kicked herself as Coulson asked, "About what?"

"About *anything.*"

She heard a buzz and glanced over at a wall-mounted security monitor wired to the camera at the front door. She crossed to it quickly and saw Rhodey standing outside. He looked up at the camera and said, "Pepper. It's Rhodey."

Pepper hit a green button beside the monitor, unlocking the door, and leaned in to the intercom speaker. "Come in."

Coulson piped up in her ear. "I'd just like to ask you a few questions."

Pepper turned in a circle, eager to get off the phone. "I'm really jammed right now. Booked solid for the next few weeks. I have to go."

She turned and gave Rhodey a small wave as he stalked into the living room, his expression grim. "Why is there a sheet of plywood on the floor back there?" Rhodey demanded, but Pepper shook her head and gestured to the phone.

"Let's just put something on the books," Coulson said doggedly. "How about"—he paused—"the twenty-eighth? At 7 PM, at Stark Industries?"

"Great," Pepper muttered, "perfect. Bye." She punched the "OFF" button.

Without further preamble, Rhodey asked, "How's he doing?"

Pepper bit her lower lip. "Not so good."

"I want to see him."

"I'm sorry, Rhodey. You can't see him right now."

Rhodey noted the way Pepper had positioned herself between him and the hallway that led to Tony's master bedroom suite. She had the air of a mother hen watching over an egg. Or maybe more like a lioness, poised to rip the hell out of anyone approaching her cub.

Rhodey looked over his shoulder at the gaping hole in the foyer ceiling, making sure Pepper saw him do it. His eyes narrowed as he faced her again. "What is going on here?" When she didn't answer him, he said quietly, "Let me in there, Pepper."

For several long moments, Pepper didn't move, facing off against Rhodey, who towered over her and outweighed her by a hundred pounds.

Then she let out a long sigh, lowered her eyes, and stepped aside. "You want to see him? *Fine.* See what you've done to him."

Rhodey started to speak, but thought better of it. Instead he hurried down the hallway to Tony's bedroom door and carefully turned the knob.

It took his eyes a few seconds to adjust to the dim

light—and then he almost wished they hadn't. Tony Stark lay in his massive bed. Tubes and wires tethered him to a bank of medical equipment at his bedside. Jarvis's robotic arm hovered nearby, watching. Tony groaned and turned his head.

Rhodey navigated his way through the various monitors and IV stands, pulled up a chair, and sat down. He had decided not to say anything else to Pepper in the hallway; now words simply refused to form in his mind, whether he wanted them to or not.

Tony drifted in and out of consciousness as Rhodey watched.

Finally Rhodey said, "Look at you. What were you thinking?"

Tony turned his head and cracked one eyelid open. The eye underneath struggled to focus, but finally came to rest on Rhodey's face. Tony swallowed hard. "Weapons I built are being used to kill innocent people," he said, barely above a whisper. "Can't let that happen anymore."

Rhodey breathed out a sigh of frustration. "You can't go around and blow up stuff every time you see something you don't like on TV."

With the specter of a smile, Tony replied, "Yes, I can."

"You got lucky! Next time they'll blow you to pieces!"

The one eye Tony had open narrowed. "Maybe next time I won't play defense."

Rhodey squeezed his own eyes shut and shook his

head. Then he got to his feet and started pacing back and forth at the foot of the bed. "Does Pepper know about this?"

Tony nodded.

Rhodey's agitation increased, tempered with genuine concern for his friend. "Tony . . . it's not like I don't understand. You know what I'm saying? I—I wish I could've been right there with you, y'know? Your heart's in the right place, no question."

Tony prompted him. "But?"

Rhodey flashed him a quick, rueful grin. "*But* I wish your methods weren't so . . . so . . . I don't even know the words, man!"

Tony coughed weakly. "Yeah, well. I've made my choice. I'm not going to sit on the sidelines anymore. I'm going to fight for what's right."

And having made that statement, before Rhodey could say anything else, Tony drifted into unconsciousness.

As Tony Stark began to snore softly, a regimented frenzy was taking place in a windowless subbasement room at the headquarters of Stark Industries.

The enormous chamber, whose function was to house part of the Reactor's coolant system, looked as if it had been forgotten, even by the people who'd constructed it. An afterthought, lost between sections of the building, its walls lined with a mad tangle of pipes. Its floor was bare concrete except for one section composed of metal grating, below which a channel of swiftly moving water created an echoing susurration that lent the entire room a certain medieval, dungeon-like air.

In the center of the room, the damaged gray armor hung in midair, again suspended from wires—but now each piece hung separately, as the suit had been "exploded," the better to examine it.

And examined it was. An elite team of Stark Industries engineers roved around it, studying it, measuring it. More engineers operated a bank of equipment lining the walls, furiously milling and machining parts.

Obadiah Stane walked among them, watching their progress. Planning.

"Civilization, gentlemen," he began, "has been preserved by the right people having the right idea at the right time. You are shaping in your hands, this very moment, the future of this company and this nation. But it is imperative this project remain data-masked, that its existence never leave these walls. Make no mistake—this is a tool that, in the wrong hands, could jeopardize civilization as we know it."

Obadiah stopped and faced the head engineer, an icy woman with a long red braid of hair down her back and eyes the color of glaciers. She spoke with a faint Eastern European accent. "Give us full access to the Sampson Cluster, and we'll have a prototype for you in record time."

Obadiah nodded once. "The Sampson's yours. We go 24-7."

Chapter Twenty-four

An icy wind howled down the mountainside, past the entrance to Raza's cave in Afghanistan, carrying with it the stink of cordite and the sickly sweet stench of burned human flesh.

Yinsen stood, the mountains behind him, his eyes sad and soulful. "Are you on the right path, Stark?" he asked. "What does your heart tell you?"

Something exploded in the distance. Men shrieked, and another explosion sounded, closer this time, then another and another, closer still, and Yinsen's torso began to bleed through his shirt.

Tony Stark woke up in his bedroom, alone.

He struggled to his elbows and caught sight of his reflection in a mirror across the room: a sad wreck of a man, hooked up to IVs and machinery that pinged and hissed.

Tony collapsed back onto the pillows, disgusted.

Several hours later, Pepper Potts slammed open the door of Tony's workshop and stared at him as he stood working on his eviscerated suit of armor. The armor hung suspended from a chain winch, about halfway disassembled, its parts fanned out around Tony on the floor and on several workbenches. Tony looked at Pepper as she stood there, his face pale but determined. Then he pointed at a modified jump drive lying nearby.

"That device will hack into Stark Industries' mainframe. I need you to go there and retrieve all shipping manifests from Obadiah's records."

Pepper took a few steps toward him and stopped, her hands on her hips. "What are you *doing*? You should be in *bed*!"

As if she hadn't said anything at all, Tony continued, "Obadiah and whoever he's working with have been dealing weapons under the table, and I'm going to stop them."

"Absolutely not," Pepper said. "I'm not helping you with anything if you're going to start this again."

Tony stopped working and leaned on the armor, staring Pepper in the eye. "There is nothing else," he said with absolute, unwavering intensity. "There's no art opening. There's no benefit. There's nothing to sign, there are no decisions to be made. There's the next mission, and nothing else. There is nothing except this."

With a heated edge to her voice, Pepper said, "I quit."

Tony raised his eyebrows a tiny fraction of an inch. "Really? You stood there by my side when all I did was reap the benefits of wholesale irresponsibility and destruction, and now that I'm trying to right those wrongs and protect the people I put in harm's way, you're going to walk out on me?"

Pepper shifted her weight and crossed her arms. "You're going to kill yourself. I can't support that."

"So far so good," he said lightly. Then, when that obviously didn't work, he added, "Pepper. I know what I have to do. I don't know if I *can,* but I know in my heart that it's right. And you do, too. And I can't do it without you."

In the subbasement coolant chamber, with the deconstructed suit of armor still hanging in the center of the room, Obadiah Stane faced off against his head engineer.

"There's no technology that can power this thing."

Obadiah frowned impatiently. "I told you: Miniaturize the ARK Reactor."

She shook her head, causing her long braid to ripple between her shoulder blades. "I'm sorry, Mr. Stane, I've tried. What you're asking for can't be done."

Obadiah's jaw clenched. "Tony Stark was able to do it in a *cave*—with a box of *scraps.*"

She shrugged apologetically. "Well . . . I'm not Tony Stark."

Obadiah glared at her, but only for a moment. Soon he turned away, his eyes distant, his mind working over a new possibility.

• • •

Many floors above the windowless room where Obadiah Stane's engineers toiled, Pepper Potts strode briskly along one of the main corridors of Stark Industries. It was about 6:45 PM, the sunlight had begun to wane, and all but a very few employees had gone home. Pepper's heels clicked so loudly on the marble floor that each footstep made her wince inwardly. She kept casting nervous glances back over her shoulder.

As quickly as she could, Pepper made her way to Tony's office, all but ran past the executive assistant's workstation, and slid into the overstuffed leather chair behind his desk. She opened Tony's custom-built Stark laptop, a portable powerhouse of a machine that was networked to every other computer in the building, including the mainframe. Wasting no time, Pepper plugged the little JumpDrive-sized device into one of the USB ports on the laptop's side.

Pepper watched the monitor, impressed despite herself, as the device began bullying its way through firewalls, passwords, and security nets—all of them set up by Obadiah Stane, and all of them falling like dominoes.

In less than a minute, the "hack drive" gained full access to the mainframe, and Pepper simply sat and watched as file after file uploaded.

Each record flashed onto the screen for a fraction of a second, and Pepper picked a few of them out one by one: Jericho missile orders, shipping manifests, delivery confirmations. The list went on and on.

"Make a copy of everything . . ." Pepper whispered.

The records kept coming up, and Pepper started seeing things that, while she didn't recognize them, still made her incredibly nervous. Schematics began flashing across the monitor, followed by blueprints. What looked like a design for a suit of armor similar to the one Tony wore, but much larger and heavier; also, a gridlike image of a room with no windows, its walls lined with pipes.

Baffled, under her breath Pepper said, "What are you *doing*, Obadiah?"

Then she turned her head sharply toward the door of the office, thinking she'd heard something. She watched, waited . . . and when she didn't hear anything else, returned to the computer.

An icon had appeared on the monitor, square with sprocket-holes up both sides: a video clip. The text beneath the icon was in Arabic. Pepper only hesitated for a moment before double-clicking on it.

The clip began playing almost immediately, grainy and raw, and Pepper gasped, horrified. It showed Tony Stark, half-dead and tied to a chair in what seemed to be a cave, with Afghan insurgents standing behind him. A banner displaying ten interlocking rings hung on the wall behind the insurgents—a banner Pepper had seen on news reports.

She had the volume muted, but the man standing beside Tony was speaking, and she felt sure it wasn't in English. Leaning close to the computer's microphone, her head shaking in disbelief, Pepper said, "Translate."

She heard a brief whir from the hard drive. Then text like subtitles appeared across the bottom of the image:

OBADIAH STANE, YOU HAVE DECEIVED US. THE PRICE TO KILL TONY STARK HAS JUST GONE UP.

Pepper gaped at the monitor, feeling as if her gut had been punched. Her hand hovered over the keyboard as she tried to decide what to do. Then she glanced up to see Obadiah Stane standing in the office doorway, watching her, and she almost screamed.

"What a nice surprise," Obadiah said.

"I . . . just wanted to get some of my personal stuff." She nodded at the monitor, trying to play it cool. Pepper couldn't tell what her voice sounded like or how her body language came off, but prayed it was at least halfway convincing. "And my résumé, just in case." She attempted a wry grin. "You know how much I love job hunting."

Obadiah stepped into the office and started to circle around the desk. Pepper switched screens, covering the download indicator with the Stark homepage, and hoped Obadiah didn't question that single click.

So far so good. He only asked, "How's Tony?"

She sat back in the chair, looking up at him. "Honestly . . . I don't know. He has shut me out."

"You and everyone else."

He moved around behind her and over to the other side of the desk again, where he picked up a framed photo of Tony Stark at a government fund-raiser, shaking hands with the governor of New Hampshire. Pepper flicked her eyes nervously at the protruding hack drive. The whir and grind of the copying files sounded as loud as an alarm in Pepper's ears.

She looked up at Obadiah again. "This . . . thing between you, it's hurting him. You're the only real father Tony ever had. It would mean so much if you could just talk—"

Obadiah shook his head and spoke matter-of-factly. "Tony's imploding. It's unfortunate . . . but you should consider whether you want to take that ride with him."

Pepper's tone turned brittle. "'Unfortunate?'"

Obadiah leaned against the edge of the desk. "You know I love Tony, but this is business. We can't save him, but we can save his legacy."

Pepper's eyes flashed over to the screen, where the download indicator was still visible at the bottom. It read "87% COMPLETED."

"It's tragic," Obadiah continued, "but Tony never really came home, did he?"

He stood and circled around behind her again, peering at the computer screen, which once again showed the Stark homepage. He sat on the edge of the desk right next to her, looking down at her with what might have been a tender expression. "This company has a bright future, Pepper. I'd like you to be a part of it."

And he reached out and gently touched her cheek with the back of his hand.

With a Herculean effort, Pepper kept her face neutral and calmly shut down the computer.

"Tony doesn't understand your value," Obadiah said. "He never did."

Pepper tried to figure out what she could possibly say, how she could possibly respond to this traitorous monster. She finally decided there was no point in tipping her hand just yet. "Are you offering me a job?" she asked sweetly.

"Think about it." He stood and moved toward the door. "Come on, I'll walk you out."

Pepper stood and, as she passed by the computer, plucked the hack drive out and palmed it. She knew he must have seen it, and since she hadn't printed out any hard copies, there was only one place her résumé could have been: on the portable drive. Still, as she followed Obadiah out of the office, she felt no desire to call further attention to it.

Obadiah stayed quiet as they made their way toward the lobby. Pepper began to wish he'd talk, since at least his voice seemed familiar, seemed like a hint of the man she had known and respected and trusted for years. Instead he stalked quietly along beside her, and her mind played on a painful loop, flashing past one landmark of betrayal after another.

Obadiah Stane, shipping missiles to Gulmira without authorization.

Obadiah Stane, establishing . . . what was it, down there in the subbasement? Some kind of secret storehouse? A clandestine research center?

Then the agonizing image, the thing so sharp she could barely let herself picture it: the translation of the grainy video. *THE PRICE TO KILL TONY STARK HAS JUST GONE UP.*

Pepper suddenly was aware that she and Obadiah were likely the only two people left in this wing of the building. He was a big man, and strong. What could she do to resist him if he decided to attack her? *Run,* that's what she could do. But what if he had locked all of the exits before coming to find her in Tony's office?

He was willing to pay to have Tony killed. What reason did she have to think he wouldn't snap her neck himself if he decided to?

The walk to the lobby seemed to get longer and longer the farther they went, and by the time they reached the staircase leading down to the front security desk, Pepper had worked herself into a veritable frenzy of anxiety, made all the worse by the need not to let it show.

But Obadiah didn't touch her, and when she reached the top of the stairs, he hung back, standing at the railing, simply watching her descend.

It occurred to her that any security guard in the building would be in Obadiah's pocket. What if he were waiting until she reached the front entrance before sending one his men to attack her? That would be more his style, she thought, than killing her with his own hands.

But as Pepper started to descend the staircase and peered down at the security desk to try to assess the situation there, she spotted someone she never expected to be this happy to see: Agent Phil Coulson.

Coulson stood at the desk, arguing with a guard there. Was that why Obadiah had hung back? Had he spotted Coulson before Pepper had? It didn't matter, she realized, as she hurried down the steps and across the lobby floor.

Coulson was so wrapped up in his argument with the guard that she surprised him when she linked arms with him, said, "Agent Coulson, imagine seeing you here!" and started dragging him toward the door.

"Miss Potts, did you forget our appointment? Seven PM?"

"No, of course not, I've been very much looking forward to it. Let's—" She glanced over her shoulder, then pushed open the door, still pulling Coulson along. "Why don't we do this somewhere else?"

Coulson allowed himself to be led out of the building.

Behind them, Obadiah Stane remained at the balcony railing, watching, expressionless.

Chapter Twenty-five

A cacophony of whirring, grinding, hissing noises filled Tony's workshop. Tony stood by the Series IX CNC Combo, looking through the plates of metal stock in the feeder bin. His color and general appearance had improved dramatically since Rhodey's visit. Of course, he still suffered from occasional blinding headaches, and Jarvis reminded him on an hourly basis that he really should still be in bed, but Tony didn't let that stop him or even slow him down much.

He wore his usual scrub pants and tank top, which he had come to think of as his workshop uniform. The blue glow of the Repulsor unit in his chest shone through the thin cotton material, an otherworldly circle above his heart.

Behind Tony, one of the many computer monitors on his workbench flashed six messages, all of them identical: "MISSED CALL—PEPPER." He hadn't turned to face the monitors for about ninety minutes, and had no idea the messages were there.

The first sign of anything unusual came when the CNC Combo suddenly powered down. Tony shot a sharp glance at the robotic arm hovering in a nearby corner. "What gives, Jarvis?"

"You have a visitor, sir," Jarvis said, speaking from every speaker in the room, as usual. "Obadiah Stane is here."

Tony bristled at the mention of Obadiah's name.

He thought of several things he'd like to say, none of them directed at Jarvis, none of them productive in even the slightest way. But all Tony said was "Thanks, Jarvis," and he turned to head upstairs.

He wanted to believe that it could all have been some colossal mistake. Obadiah had lost faith in him, yes, and had gone behind his back to try to force him out of the company. That was one thing. But the arms shipments—Tony clung to the thought that maybe he was wrong. Maybe there was some other factor he didn't know about. Maybe Obadiah wasn't the monster he seemed to be.

Tony walked into the living room and found Obadiah there, holding a pizza box.

"I just had it flown in from Chicago," the older man said. He didn't sound openly hostile.

Tony leaned against the door-frame and folded his arms across his chest. His anger fluctuated in intensity minute to minute, sometimes second to second, but it never left completely.

Understanding that Tony wasn't going to volunteer anything, Obadiah nodded and put the pizza box down on the coffee table. Then he crossed to Tony and handed him an envelope. "I'd like you to proofread something for me."

Jarvis's voice emanated from the living room's sound system. "Would you like me to spell-check it, sir?"

Obadiah made a face and said, "Can you turn him off? All the way?"

Tony had opened the envelope and taken out a one-page letter, which he now scanned, his eyebrows drawing together. Still reading, he said, "Spin down, Jarvis."

"Understood, sir," Jarvis replied. "Spinning down." A small *pop* from the speakers was the only audible indication that the massive AI had indeed gone offline, but Obadiah seemed satisfied.

Tony finally looked up from the letter. "Your resignation."

Obadiah nodded again slowly, as if a great burden rested on his shoulders. "You were right. It's not my company—not my name on the building. We were a great team . . . but I guess this is where our paths diverge."

A polite noise, something like "*blip,*" sounded from a nearby wall-mounted security panel, right beside one of Tony's favorite easy chairs. Tony stepped over to it and saw the words "INCOMING—PEPPER POTTS" scroll across the small screen.

"Pepper," he said to Obadiah. "I should take that."

A pained look crossed his former mentor's face.

"Tony. Please. I'll be out of here in a minute."

Tony wavered, his hand hovering near the control panel, warring with the decision . . . but finally he acquiesced. The push of a button sent Pepper's call to voice mail.

Obadiah took a step closer to Tony. Everything that Tony had always loved about him was right there, right on the surface: the fatherly nature, the good-humored, laughing eyes, the easy, forgiving smile.

"We have too much history to part on bad terms," Obadiah said, and put an affectionate hand on Tony's shoulder. "I'd like your blessing."

Tony started to answer and his eyes went wide in sudden, overwhelming agony.

As Tony stiffened and began to lose his balance, Obadiah adjusted the filter-plugs in his own ears. Then he reached out with one hand and shoved Tony backward. Tony fell gracelessly onto his easy chair.

Obadiah set the sonic Taser down on a small end table beside the chair, still activated and aimed carefully at Tony's ear. Then he knelt and ripped Tony's tank top open, exposing the glowing Repulsor unit. "Easy now," he said. "Try to breathe."

Tony tried to make a sound, any sound, but couldn't. His eyes flickered and bulged, watering with pain as the taser drilled into his skull.

Obadiah kept talking. "You can't mess with progress, Tony. It's an insult to the gods. You created your greatest weapon ever, but you think that means it belongs to *you*. It doesn't, Tony. It belongs to the *world*."

Obadiah reached into a pocket of his suit and pulled out what could have passed for a miniature tire iron. The tool gleamed like surgical steel.

Moving a bit clumsily, unsure of how it should go but nevertheless determined to see it through, Obadiah Stane began prying the Repulsor unit out of Tony's chest.

"Your 'heart' will be the seed of the next generation of weapons. They'll help us steer the world back in the right direction—put the balance of power back in our hands. The *right* hands."

With a tiny grunt, Obadiah popped the Repulsor unit loose. Its blue glow reflected in his face as he raised it closer.

"By the time you die, my prototype will be operational." He grinned down at Tony. "It's not as conservative as yours. Soon we'll have an army of them."

Obadiah stood up and wrapped the Repulsor unit in a large white handkerchief. Then he picked up the sonic Taser, clicked it off, and dropped it in a pocket.

The unbearable agony finally gone, Tony groaned and half-rolled, half-fell out of his chair onto the floor, where he landed faceup, staring at the ceiling.

"The sad thing is," Obadiah said as he prepared to leave, "we're both the good guys."

He killed the lights on his way out, leaving Tony Stark all alone and dying.

In his office at Edwards Air Force Base, Rhodey frowned as he listened to Pepper talking on the phone.

"What do you mean, he paid to have Tony killed? Slow down . . . why would Obadiah—" He broke off, concentrating. It didn't take long for Pepper to convince him. Jumping to his feet, Rhodey demanded, "Where is Tony now?"

In the underground parking garage of Agent Phil Coulson's office building, Pepper, Coulson, and five more dark-suited agents walked with urgency toward a couple of dark sedans. Pepper had her earpiece in, her face creased with worry as she spoke to Rhodey.

"I don't know, he's not answering his phone. Will you just go over there and check on him?"

"You bet I will," Rhodey said on the other end of the line. "Where are *you*?"

Pepper glanced at the dour men accompanying her. She had followed Agent Coulson here to his office, where it had taken her a great deal more time than she was comfortable with to convince him of everything. "I'm in transit," Pepper said. "Just, just let me know if he's okay, would you? Thanks, Rhodey."

She hung up. The agents started to pile into black sedans, and Agent Coulson held a door open for her, but Pepper walked past him and made a beeline for her own car parked nearby.

"I know a shortcut," she called out over her shoulder.

Coulson looked from Pepper to the agent behind the wheel and back. "I'll ride with her," he said, and hurried over to jump into Pepper's car.

Wasting no time, Pepper threw the vehicle into gear and squealed out of the parking garage. The sedans filled with SHIELD agents did their best to keep up.

Tony Stark pushed open the door to his workshop and flopped inside, crawling painfully across the floor. He was almost done. Running on fumes. And he knew it. Tony had one last chance and it was that chance he struggled to reach now: the dimly glowing original Repulsor unit that Pepper had mounted in a Lucite box.

The box rested on a table at one end of a workbench. Tony could barely move, much less stand up, and had no chance of reaching it; the best he could do was to bump the table's closest leg with his shoulder. It was a weak, pathetic effort, but he kept it up, jarring the table again and again.

Tony nearly passed out from pain and shock when the box fell and broke open on the concrete floor right next to his head. His hand trembled as he picked up the glowing blue disk.

Pepper Potts, Agent Coulson, and the five other agents stopped outside the ARK Reactor building, facing a rear door.

"You're sure it's in here?" Coulson asked.

Pepper shot him a black look and punched in the door code. The heavy door opened obligingly. "It's in here," she snapped. "I saw the blueprints. And the next door won't open that easily."

"Don't you worry about that," Coulson told her. "Just show us the way."

Pepper led the men inside, bypassed the Reactor itself, and headed down a side corridor to a maintenance hallway. Halfway down the hall, she stopped at a much heavier-looking door. "This is it," she said. "Whatever's behind here isn't supposed to be."

Coulson nodded to the other men. One of them moved in and began applying detonator cord to the door hinges, while the rest of the group moved far enough back down the corridor to be safe. Soon the last agent joined them, said, "Clear," and hit a small clacker.

The door's hinges disintegrated in the blast, and the door itself, knocked out of its frame, slammed to the floor. Coulson led the group back to the doorway and through it, into a short hallway that ended in a set of stairs leading down.

Chapter Twenty-six

The front door of Tony Stark's mansion split down the middle and sagged off its hinges with the force of Rhodey's kick.

Rhodey charged inside, flipping on lights, searching for Tony. He spotted signs of struggle in the living room—objects knocked over, things broken—and followed the trail to the door leading down to Tony's workshop.

"Tony? *Tony!* Where are you?"

Rhodey ran down the steps, and went into Tony's workshop, which he hadn't seen since Tony had first begun working on the powered armor. He paused, staring around him, taking in the Mark II armor hanging on a rack . . . the schematics, components, and prototype armor pieces lying everywhere . . . the weaponized, fully restored red-and-gold Mark III armor, mounted on another rack . . . and Tony, sitting in his "surgery chair," Jarvis's robotic arm making adjustments to the glowing Repulsor unit in Tony's chest.

Rhodey moved closer. "Tony?"

Tony Stark stood up. Healthy again, strong, and looking coldly, dangerously angry. "Obadiah tried to kill me," he said, and Rhodey almost recoiled from the whip-crack sound of his friend's voice.

Pepper, Coulson, and the other five agents reached the room Pepper had seen in the blueprints in Obadiah Stane's file, but they proceeded with great uncertainty for two reasons.

First, the room was about three times bigger than Pepper had realized. It was cavernous, almost the size of a small airplane hangar, and thick with dense shadows.

Second, moving through it was like moving through some kind of insane, homicidal carnival fun house. The place was a jungle of vats, huge milling machines, and what appeared to be pieces of a gigantic suit of armor.

They turned a corner and came face-to-face with the reassembled gray "Mark I" armor. They stopped, a little spooked, the Mark I's blank eyeholes staring at them menacingly.

"What's that framework supposed to do?" one of the agents asked, pointing at a massive, empty steel rack at the far end of the room.

No one answered him.

Coulson gestured to the team. They fanned out to search more efficiently.

Long moments passed, tension mounting second by

second, as they made their way through the darkness.

The agent who had asked about the huge steel rack was named Sun, a tall, solidly built man of Korean descent. Agent Sun had moved close to the north wall of the room, away from the rest of the group, his gun out and ready.

The gun did him little good as something metallic clamped around his neck and jerked him completely off his feet and into the shadows.

In Tony's workshop, Rhodey found himself at a loss for words. He had watched as Tony systematically encased himself in the red-and-gold armor—the suit Tony referred to as the Mark III—and now the only piece left was the helmet. Tony stood in front of him, a streamlined metal juggernaut, and Rhodey could actually feel the power radiating off of the suit.

Finally his tongue limbered up enough to ask, "What's the plan?"

"I'm going after Stane," Tony said matter-of-factly, as if that explained everything. After a second's thought, Rhodey decided it actually *did* explain everything.

"I'm right behind you."

Tony turned and made his way farther into the workshop, positioning himself under the hole in the ceiling. He nodded. "I'm counting on it."

Tony lowered the helmet over his head and it automatically sealed tight against the suit's collar. Then he powered up the propulsion boots and blasted off straight up through the hole in the ceiling, knocking it even wider as he went.

Rhodey stared after him, impressed all the way down to his bones and envious. He turned and eyed the Mark II armor, considering for a moment.

"Next time, baby," he said.

For now, Rhodey decided to take advantage of the next best thing. He sprinted back into the garage, hopped into a sports car, and laid rubber on the concrete as he took off after Tony.

Pepper Potts wandered the western edge of the coolant chamber, looking for Obadiah Stane. She pulled out her cell phone and attempted to make a call, but the phone got no service at all down here.

Ahead of her the pipes and girders got particularly thick . . . and she squinted, unsure of what she was seeing.

Were those two glowing spots?

Eyes?

Suddenly the whole tangle shook as the hissing of hydraulics joined the groan of grinding metal, and then gunfire rang out, bullets ricocheting everywhere. Several of the rounds hit pipes protruding from the wall, causing huge, scalding jets of steam to blast out into the room.

The resulting clouds of water vapor further obscured any trace of what Pepper might have seen, but the gunfire didn't stop, and Pepper turned and ran from the pandemonium.

Wheeling, she squinted through the steam and the

smoke, trying to see through the profusion of machine gears between her and whatever was going on. Agents screamed and ran, darting this way and that, trying to find some cover. Behind them, an enormous, monstrous shadow flitted in and out of sight.

As she watched, an agent emerged from the steam, stopped to try to reload his gun, and was yanked back into the vapor clouds by an unseen force.

Pepper turned and ran again, desperate to find a way out. She screamed as a ragged piece of metal flashed by her, less than an inch from her right ear, and cut through more pipes as it embedded itself in the concrete wall.

Another agent stumbled out of the murk, clutching his radio. "Agents down! Agents down!" He blinked, focusing his eyes on Pepper, and when he realized who she was he shouted, *"Get out of here!"* The agent rushed forward, grabbed her arm, and half-pushed, half-dragged her toward the exit.

From behind them in the steam came the sound of something incredibly heavy moving, accompanied by a tremor in the floor, and the agent turned and ran toward it, firing into the obscuring mists.

The agent's sense of direction turned out to be a bit better than Pepper's, as she realized he had guided her to a spot only a few feet away from the door that led back upstairs. She took the stairs two at a time, but paused halfway up when the concussive sound she had heard seconds before came again and again, resolving itself into footsteps that were coming closer. Pepper couldn't help staring down at the doorway just as something crashed into it. It took Pepper a second to process what she was seeing: Someone in a gigantic armored suit clawed and scraped at the doorway, reaching one titanic arm up the stairs and grasping for her, but the armor was too big. She only had fractured glimpses of it—the arm and part of the chest—but she immediately recognized the glowing blue circle set in the center of the suit's chest plate, and her own heart froze over as she realized what that could mean.

"Come back, Pepper," a modulated, inhuman voice bellowed from the huge metal construct below her. "Let me show you what I've done."

"Who are you?" Pepper whispered.

"Tony Stark's an Iron Man?" A colossal fist smashed into the stairs and almost made Pepper fall. "Now it's time for Iron Monger."

The armored giant struggled and raked and ground away at the cement, debris showering down as it slowly but steadily smashed its way into the stairwell. Pepper turned and dashed up the stairs as quickly as her legs would take her.

The hallways inside the ARK Reactor building sped past in a blur as Pepper sprinted toward the outer exit, and she felt a burst of elation as she made it outside, slamming the door behind her. With that monstrosity trapped, she had a hope of calling in some sort of help.

Her fingers shook badly as she opened her cell phone, but Tony's number was set to one-touch, so the call went through immediately. She gasped, relieved beyond measure when he answered.

"Pepper?"

"Tony! Thank God I got ahold of you. Listen to me. Obadiah went crazy. And there's someone in a big suit, it's kind of like yours—"

"Pepper, hang on, hang on a minute. Where are you?"

She took a breath to answer him, but cut the breath short when she heard a low, thunderous noise and felt the ground tremble beneath her feet. She managed to cry, "Tony!" Then the asphalt cracked and buckled not six feet from where she stood, and Iron Monger's gigantic fist punched up into the night air.

The impact knocked Pepper off her feet, and the cell phone and earpiece both skittered away from her.

Like a hatching dinosaur, Iron Monger crunched and ripped his way up from below, peeling the asphalt away as he pulled himself out of the ground. Finally he planted his feet and rose to his full height, and Pepper gasped, terrified.

The suit of armor looked in many ways like the much smaller one Pepper had seen in the subbasement, but expanded in every way. It towered over her, ten feet tall at least, maybe twelve, a gunmetal gray behemoth. A Gatling gun mounted on its shoulder whirred, barrels spinning, and rockets protruded from multiple launch bays. The blank surface of the faceplate and the dead, merciless eyes bore down on her as Iron Monger took a step toward her, then another. Hands the size of car tires flexed their fingers, reaching for her.

Pepper scrambled to her feet and backed away, afraid to turn her back on this beast, and when her foot struck her cell phone she bent and grabbed it up.

Too late, she realized she had put herself between Iron Monger and the wall of the ARK Reactor building. She had nowhere to run.

Pepper thumbed the "SPEAKER" button on the phone, hoping Tony might still be on the line, not knowing what she might say to him but not wanting to be alone when the giant metal hands crushed her.

"Tony," she said weakly. Tony's voice came from the phone with an urgency she hadn't expected: "Pepper, I have one thing to say to you: *Duck!*"

Pepper's eyes went wide, and she flattened herself to the ground, just as Tony came blazing out of the sky in a ballistic streak of red and gold borne on a plume of blue flame. He brought his gauntlets forward, palms out, and unleashed hellish twin Repulsor blasts that hit Iron Monger so hard the giant actually came off the ground.

Tony followed up this strike by plowing into the monstrosity with both fists. The two armored combatants smashed into and straight through the wall of the building, disappearing from sight, but Pepper heard the crashes and destruction as they broke through the floor.

She stood and stumbled to the gaping hole they had created, peered inside, and gasped. The monstrous force of Tony's attack had driven Iron Monger through two more security walls before smashing him down to a lower level. Now Pepper could see from the outside of the building straight through to the core of the ARK Reactor and as she watched, the transparent shield housing of the Reactor began to crack.

Klaxons blared as red lights flashed all around her. "The ARK Reactor core has been breached," a calm, feminine voice announced over a loudspeaker. "All personnel evacuate immediately."

Chapter Twenty-seven

Tony became disoriented for a couple of seconds as he and the gray stranger crashed through walls and floors, descending, smashing through reinforced concrete in a mad, chaotic tangle.

Their descent finally stopped, at least partially, when they broke through the ceiling of the subbasement coolant chamber. Tony tumbled along the metal grating in the floor; Iron Monger crunched through the grating, bursting more pipes as he fell, and disappeared into the rushing water below.

Tony got to his feet, looking around at what was left of the enormous room; the shock wave of their impact had sent everything in the room crashing to the floor. Gouts of steam still sprayed everywhere, turning the whole place into a confusing, hazard-filled junkyard. He tentatively reactivated his cell link and said, "Pepper?"

"Tony!" Her words crackled with static. "Are you okay?"

He looked up at the ceiling of the coolant chamber, more steam hissing from a multitude of broken pipes and tubes. "We've got big problems, Pepper. The ARK Reactor is melting down."

"I know! It just blew up!"

"No, it didn't. When it blows up, it's going to take the whole city with it."

After a tiny pause, Pepper said, "Well, that makes me feel better."

"The only way to prevent a meltdown is to overload the Reactor and discharge the excess power."

"How are you going to do that?"

Tony moved over to the smashed grating and scanned the surface of the water below. Not for a second did he believe that getting dunked would put the enemy armor out of action. "*You're* going to do that."

Pepper's voice rose in pitch. "Me?"

"Yes. I want you to go to the central control panel—"

Even higher: "You want me to go *in there*?"

"It's a clean power source, Pepper, you know that. It's not like you're going to get radiation poisoning."

"No, no, I might just get blown to smithereens! That's much more comforting!"

"You won't get blown to smithereens if you do what I tell you. Now go to the panel and close all the low-voltage relays. Then I need you to go to the east wall and close all the 800-amp breakers."

"I don't know what you're talking about!"

Tony hesitated. Was that a ripple in the water? He

switched to thermal scan, but it showed nothing, just the cool blue of the stream in the channel. "Pepper, just turn on all of the little switches, then turn on all of the big switches."

"Turn them on?" Pepper was fast approaching panic. "I thought you wanted me to close them? Tony? You want me to close them or turn them on?"

Tony broke off from answering Pepper at the sound of a crunching, collapsing rumble from elsewhere in the room. He swung around, trying to pinpoint the source, but the thermal scan registered all of the steam plumes in brilliant red, throwing the whole image into a confusing jumble.

A booming voice reached him, echoing hollowly around the room, impossible to pinpoint. "Trying to rid the world of weapons, you gave it the best one ever."

Tony took a step forward. "This wasn't meant for the world." He searched around him, staring into every possible hiding place, trying to penetrate the clouds of steam. Anything consuming as much power as that armor should show up like a neon sign.

"How can you be so selfish?" the voice continued. "Do you understand what you've created? This will put the balance of power back in our hands for *decades*. Your country needs this."

"What kind of world will it be when everybody's got one?"

"Your father helped give us the bomb. What kind of world would it be if he'd failed us?"

Tony slowly skirted a pile of wreckage, alert, ready for anything . . . except for the thermal dampeners built into the other armor. In a heartbeat Tony realized he'd missed the enormous battle suit because its surface temperature regulated itself to blend in with its surroundings. Only now, when it ramped up to full-motion activity, did the colossal machine flare into blood-red, and it was far too late for Tony to react as Iron Monger charged him.

Viselike hands closed around Tony's torso as the two of them smashed into the coolant chamber's wall with the force of a bullet train. The cement of the wall exploded into powder as they drove through it, then tunneled through twenty feet of earth and burst out into open air.

It was a mere tenth of a second before they slammed into the side of a speeding tractor-trailer, ripped completely through the cargo compartment and out the other side, and crash-landed onto the surface of the freeway that passed by Stark Industries' headquarters.

Vehicles swerved, wove, and crunched into each other as the two armored warriors struggled to their feet. A hydrogen-powered, twin-sectioned bus jammed on its brakes, its rear section jackknifing as it whipped around Iron Monger, narrowly avoiding a head-on collision.

Pepper's voice sprang into Tony's ear, desperate. "Tony, I need some help here! I closed all the things . . ."

Tony smashed a fist into Iron Monger's side. It felt

like punching a truck with his bare hand. "Go to the TR1 box," he said, critically distracted, "and hit the red button."

Inside the ARK Reactor's core chamber, distressingly close to the huge pool of superheated plasmic liquid, Pepper sprinted along a metal catwalk until she came to a panel with "TR1" stenciled on its cover. Twenty feet away, the enormous, pulsing blue core spire blazed with harsh light that hurt Pepper's eyes even when she shut them tightly. She grabbed the cover and flipped it open and saw a bank of eighteen buttons inside. All of them were red. All of them were flashing.

"Thanks, Tony," she muttered.

Iron Monger got to his feet first. He reached behind him, grabbed a station wagon with a stunned mother and two children inside, and picked it up off the freeway. The sound of screams from the station wagon blended eerily with the chorus of car horns as vehicles backed up farther and farther.

Tony rose, holding out his hands in a placating gesture. "Don't! This is *our* fight!"

"People are always going to die," the voice rumbled from the depths of the suit. "It's part of the chess game."

Immediately Tony raised his gauntlets and triggered both of the palm Repulsor emitters.

Nothing happened. He realized the brutal punishment he'd taken going through the wall must have damaged a connection somewhere, but he spent no time thinking about it. Instead he snapped, "Emergency power!"

The mother and children screamed louder as Iron Monger stepped forward, lining them up to drive Tony into the ground like a tent peg.

In Tony's ear, Jarvis said, "Sir, you'll drain the—" but Tony screamed, *"Now!"* and for just an instant the entire world turned a painful blue-white.

The Repulsor blast exploded from Tony's chest, caught Iron Monger point-blank, and knocked him completely off the freeway just as he brought the station wagon down in a vicious arc. Tony sprang forward and caught the car, slowing it down enough so that the impact wouldn't hurt the passengers, but the last of his power faded before he could set it back down on the concrete. The car thudded to the earth, pinning a suddenly helpless Tony underneath it.

The mother inside the car needed a moment to understand that she and her children were safe; it was a moment cut very short as the ground trembled with Iron Monger's footsteps, coming back toward them.

One of the kids screamed, *"Go, Mom! Go!"* and the mother hit the gas pedal. The wagon sprang forward, skidding and weaving as it sped away from Iron Monger, but Tony remained pinned underneath,

240

dragged along in a shower of sparks.

Iron Monger bellowed and came after them, moving faster and faster, and began using cars as stepping stones, each step covering more and more distance.

On another part of the L.A. freeway system, Rhodey whipped through traffic, driving like hell and leaning on his horn. Taillights flashed past like tracers as he slalomed through the vehicles around him.

With a grunt and a heave, Tony finally managed to push the vehicle off of him. It lurched and bounced as if it had just hit the world's biggest speed bump, but continued on its way, leaving only a dislodged muffler behind. The children inside stared out the back window at Tony as the car disappeared.

Tony staggered to his feet, then both heard and felt the now-familiar tremors as Iron Monger bore down on him. He wondered if maybe his gauntlet Repulsors would work now, but he didn't get the chance to find out.

Just as Iron Monger caught up with Tony, a grizzled biker on a classic motorcycle wove around a truck, trying to make his way through all of the snarled traffic. The biker spotted Iron Monger, realized he had just put himself in the wrong place at the wrong time, and tried to veer away, but the giant reached out and grabbed the bike's front wheel.

As the unfortunate biker somersaulted away, arms

and legs pinwheeling, Iron Monger brought the motor-cycle around in a brutal swing and sent Tony flying like a football at kickoff.

In the ARK Reactor's core chamber, Pepper stared at the central control panel where a number of indicator bars were rising steadily into the red. She shouted into the cell phone, not knowing if Tony could hear her, desperate for some sort of help. "Tony! It's not looking good here! I could really use some guidance right about now!"

She got no response.

Tony landed in a rolling, clanging heap, and finally came to rest in front of the previously jackknifing bus, which now stood parked, blocked in by cars that Iron Monger had demolished in his pursuit of Tony.

At the sight of Tony's arrival, the passengers and driver all bolted, scattering away from the bus and diving off the freeway. Passengers and drivers in the surrounding cars saw this and followed suit, so that when Iron Monger caught up with Tony again, they were the only two people around.

Iron Monger descended from the sky on twin pillars of Repulsor flame the size of tree trunks. Tony raised one hand, trying to target again, but the connection was still broken. His gauntlet Repulsor emitters were dead.

Iron Monger raised one foot and blasted Tony with an inferno of Repulsor propulsion. Tony struggled, trying to get away but unable to move.

Finally the propulsion jet cut off and Iron Monger took a step backward. Tony seized the opportunity and shouted, "The ARK Reactor is going to explode! A lot of people are going to die!"

But it was as if Tony hadn't said anything at all. The villain came forward again and drew back an enormous fist, about to slam it down onto Iron Man in an impact that Tony knew would crush him into the pavement.

Suddenly, Iron Monger was distracted by the sound of a rapidly approaching vehicle.

Tony cranked his head around just enough to see his own car, with Rhodey behind the wheel, come rocketing down the breakdown lane, its engine red-lined. The car slammed straight into Iron Monger's leg, crumpled up, and spun off to the side like the flimsiest of toys. The impact knocked the gray giant off-balance, and before he could correct it, Iron Monger pitched forward and crushed a hydrogen-powered bus, ripping it open right down to the fuel tanks. One of the flailing metal hands brushed up against an exposed sparkplug.

Hellfire erupted as the hydrogen tanks ignited in Iron Monger's face and a white-hot fireball enveloped him. Tony groaned, his skin blistering in places as the flames washed over him, and rolled over to his hands and knees. He stumbled away from the conflagration, went to his ruined car, and ripped the roof away with his hands.

Rhodey looked up at him, coughing from the gases released by the now-deflated airbag.

"You had to take my car," Tony said dryly.

Rhodey coughed again and stood up through the newly made sunroof. Both of them turned to look at the inferno that used to be a bus. Nothing moved there at all; in fact, it was difficult to tell, at this point, that what they were looking at used to *be* a bus. Through the flames, it seemed to be little more than a heap of molten metal.

Tony turned back to Rhodey and said, "Get this area evacuated! There's going to be a meltdown!"

Rhodey opened his mouth to say, *"Meltdown?"* but before he could, Tony ignited his propulsion boots and shot into the sky, zooming back to Stark Industries.

Watching Tony go, Rhodey shouted, "You could have said 'Thank you!'"

Then he pulled out his cell phone and started dialing.

Chapter Twenty-eight

Zooming across the L.A. skyline, Tony waited until the ringing in his ears had subsided, then called Pepper back on the cell link. "Pepper? How's it going?"

"I did everything you told me to," she said. Tony felt for her, as he recognized the combination of terror and tension in her words. "It's still telling me, 'Circuit Not Complete.'"

He nodded. "All right. I've got to get to the roof. Sit tight."

He thought he heard Pepper snort before he broke the connection. It only took seconds to get to the ARK Reactor building, which was now impossible to miss thanks to the brilliant blue light shining out from every window. Random blue energy arcs flashed across the building's exterior. Tony landed amid a small forest of satellite dishes mounted on the Reactor's roof.

He activated the thermal filter in his heads-up display. That took him straight to a cable running just below the roof's surface; he used his hands to pull the roof apart until he exposed the cable, which he then ripped in half and attached to one of the satellite dishes.

Blue bolts of power crackled up the cable and began playing across the dish's surface.

"Pepper, are you there?"

"Yes! What's going on?"

"I'm about to complete the circuit. Once I do, it's going to discharge all the power and channel it up through the roof. Get ready to push the Emergency Master Bypass. Do you see that?"

Silence, as Pepper looked. "Yeah, I've got it. I feel like I know this control panel better than I know my cell phone now."

"Well, when I tell you, throw that switch—but not until I'm off the roof. It's going to fry everything up here."

"Okay. Just tell me when."

Tony eyed the cable's connection to the antenna. Not satisfied with its security, he disengaged one of his gauntlets and used it as a clamp, holding the cable steady.

"Tony! Whatever you did, the panel's telling me, 'Circuit Complete' now!"

"Good, good, now hold off till I get clear, then hit the button."

Tony waited for Pepper to acknowledge what he had just said, but any words she might have spoken were lost in a cataclysmic *boom* as Iron Monger landed

246

on the roof behind Tony, flames still licking from his blackened armor. Pepper asked, "Tony, what was that noise?" but he couldn't answer as Iron Monger nailed Tony with a mammoth roundhouse punch.

Tony skidded across the rooftop, but spun around and triggered the propulsion boots, rocketing to retaliate. Tony zeroed in on the hydraulic system that enabled the massive battle-suit's movement, intending to rip it apart, but he hadn't counted on Iron Monger reacting quite so quickly.

The villain grabbed Tony out of the air, locked him in a massive bear hug, and began tightening his grip.

Pepper shouted, "Tony! Tony, are you—" but the connection popped and went dead.

Tony felt the shell of his armor begin to crack. The heads-up display that had saved his life so many times started splintering. He felt one of his ribs break.

Desperate, Tony activated the chaff hatch. Instantly a tiny explosive charge propelled the packet of metallic strips out and back, where they bounced off the roof and surrounded both men in a blinding, twisting cloud of glinting metal.

Surprised and confused, Iron Monger lost his grip on Tony and stumbled backward, trying to regain his field of vision. When the chaff strips finally settled on the roof, Tony was nowhere to be seen.

"It's pointless to hide!" Iron Monger bellowed. "Running will only prolong the inevitable!"

"I couldn't agree more," Tony said, as he landed squarely on Iron Monger's back with the force of an antitank missile. Iron Monger staggered forward, thrown off-balance, and Tony put that disorientation to good use. Wedging his one gauntleted hand between two of the gray suit's back plates, Tony grabbed a thick electrical column and pulled.

"You know," he grunted, as Iron Monger's suit began twitching spasmodically, "it might not have been the wisest course of action, trying to kill me with a suit built from my own designs." Tony wrenched the cable loose, ripping it free as if pulling out a spinal cord.

"That took care of your HUD, didn't it?" Tony said, digging around for another vulnerable component. "Let's see you try to hit anything now."

One of Iron Monger's arms whipped up and back, and the gigantic hand clamped squarely around Tony's head. Tony struggled and tried to break free, but he couldn't get enough leverage.

"I don't have to hit anything when I can just tear your head off," Iron Monger growled, his voice distorted and demonic. Then he slammed his arm forward again, trying to break Tony's neck.

It didn't work as planned, but it had an effect nonetheless: Tony flew across the rooftop, sliding and bouncing in a flailing mess. And Iron Monger still held Tony's helmet in his hand.

Tony smashed completely through one of the satellite dishes before he came to a full stop. He groaned, tried to get up on one elbow, but collapsed back to the roof.

Iron Monger moved forward slowly, as if to savor the moment. He brought his hands together and crushed Tony's helmet between them. Then he raised one arm, bringing the Gatling gun to bear and faltered. The gun wavered, unable to find a target. In frustration, he finally unleashed a random barrage of bullets.

The rounds slammed into the roof, digging through it like the blade of a chain saw, and the structure collapsed underneath Tony, who was barely able to grab onto an exposed girder to keep from falling.

A vast space opened up below Tony. He hung from the girder directly above the ARK Reactor core, and stared straight down into the bubbling, superheated plasma pool at its heart. He spotted Pepper, standing on the metal catwalk. She saw him and screamed.

Tony yelled down to Pepper, "Hit the button! Pepper, hit the button!"

He could see her down there, her hand on the Master Bypass. "You said not to!"

Tony threw himself flat and rolled away from the hole as Iron Monger fired two rockets at him. With his heads-up display gone, the villain could only guess at how to aim his weapons.

"Just do it!" Tony screamed.

Still she hesitated. "Are you off the roof?"

He rolled, dodging two more rockets. The first two had blazed straight out into the ocean, but these flashed past Tony and slammed into the wall of the next building over, their impacts and immediate explosions making Tony's ears ring worse than ever.

"Pepper, we don't have a choice! We have to stop him! Do it now!"

Below on the catwalk, Pepper bit her lip and hit the Master switch, then dove under the control console as the air turned steel-blue. A wave of electromagnetic energy flashed upward along the Reactor's core spire, swelling as it traveled. When it hit the roof, it paused for several long, agonizing moments—as if it were trapped amid the satellite dishes—while the unleashed Repulsor energy vaporized most of the roof.

Then an electromagnetic pulse flashed out in all directions, turning both Tony and Iron Monger into statues as it shut down all of their power and electronics. It continued rolling out from Stark headquarters, blanketing the entirety of Los Angeles and leaving perfect darkness in its wake.

What was left of the roof of the ARK Reactor building sagged dangerously. The two iron giants both remained at the edge, frozen, powerless. Tony glanced down at the Repulsor unit in his chest.

It was dead, too.

Iron Monger was closer to the edge of the hole than Tony, and as Tony watched, the much larger battle-suit toppled over and began sliding toward the hole. One frozen, outstretched hand caught on a seam in the roof and halted its motion, though only barely.

Rather than save himself, the man inside the armor shifted slightly, trying to aim one of the suit's guns at Tony. But the small movement dislodged Iron

Monger's frozen hand from the seam in the roof that had held it in place.

The huge suit of armor began sliding again, quickly picked up speed, and disappeared over the edge of the hole in the roof.

The tanklike battle suit plummeted through the Reactor's core silo and fell directly into the plasma pool, which hissed and swallowed it up.

The pool continued bubbling and seething, showing no trace that Iron Monger had ever existed.

On the roof, Tony lay motionless and let his eyes slowly close. He stayed that way, waiting for the end. Waiting for the moment when the shrapnel would finally pierce his heart and end the life he still wanted to live: the life that he could use to do so much more good. He tried not to let regret overwhelm his last moments.

Then two beams of light hit his face and made him open his eyes again. He squinted and saw Pepper and Rhodey running toward him across the remains of the roof, both of them holding flashlights.

Tony felt a surge of intense relief before he let himself pass out.

Epilogue

The following day, while a newly hired team of engineers worked nonstop on repairing the ARK Reactor, Tony and Pepper walked side by side down a hallway in the Stark Industries administrative building. Pepper held a stack of newspapers in her arms, along with her tablet computer and a bound sheaf of papers, but she handled the load with grace. Her appearance was impeccable, as usual, her hair swept up into a smooth, trendy style and her clothing immaculate.

Tony's clothes were also immaculate, since Pepper had had them delivered that morning, but his face bore evidence of the punishment he'd taken, and he walked with a slight limp. Every now and then he touched the Repulsor unit in his chest, its light hidden beneath several layers of clothing but its warmth comforting.

Pepper shoved the sheaf of papers into Tony's hands. "Here, your alibi. You were on your yacht. I've got port papers that put you in Avalon all night, and sworn statements from fifty of your guests."

He flipped through the papers. "Maybe it was just the two of us. On the yacht, I mean."

"Focus, please."

Silently Tony reached over and pulled the top newspaper out of the stack Pepper carried. It was the current *L.A. Times*, and the headline blared out, "WHO IS IRON MAN?" Below the header was a grainy photo of Tony and Iron Monger, locked in battle on the roof of the ARK Reactor.

"'Iron Man,'" Tony said musingly. "Not technically accurate, since it's mostly carbon-fiber and ceramic. But I like the ring of it."

They reached the lobby and Tony stopped, his expression thoughtful. Pepper stopped, too, looking at him questioningly.

"You know . . ." he said, "that night at the concert hall. Do you ever think about it?"

Pepper looked into his eyes for a long moment, and Tony thought he could see—was *sure* he could see— her perfect composure start to fade. He edged closer to her, just a tiny bit, and drank in the sight of her clear, flawless blue eyes.

Then, with a touch of sadness in her voice, Pepper said, "I don't know what you're talking about, Mr. Stark." She shifted the stack of papers enough to reach up and straighten his necktie. Not meeting his eyes. All business. Stepping back, she asked, "Will that be all, Mr. Stark?"

Tony kept his face perfectly calm, even though a small, icy knot had just tightened painfully in his heart.

Tony looked away and saw Rhodey waiting for him in the lobby. He turned back to Pepper and nodded.

"That will be all, Miss Potts."

Pepper watched Tony walk away in silence. Then she turned and went back to work.